CW01481476

THE EXECUTIONER

To Jayne. lots of love

Des

xx

THE EXECUTIONER

Desmond McGrath

ATHENA PRESS
LONDON

THE EXECUTIONER
Copyright © Desmond McGrath 2009

ISBN 978 1 84748 593 9

First published 2009 by
ATHENA PRESS
Queen's House, 2 Holly Road
Twickenham TW1 4EG
United Kingdom

Printed for Athena Press

To Ella, my latest grandchild and the inspiration for the boat
Ellabella. *And Elaine, my friend and number one fan. Love you.*
And most especially my wife Barbara, for putting up with all my
moods and tantrums while writing the book.

Observe life. Observe people, observe situations and listen to dialogue. Capture emotions and try to put them down on paper.
   Then be great.

Desmond McGrath, 2008

Acknowledgements

Thanks to Pete Dawes and John Lyons for their help and ideas with the Villa Park chapters.

Thanks to my friends at Villa Park, especially Tony the stadium manager for the coffee and choccy biscuits and the freedom to roam the ground when it was closed to do my research and locations.

And thanks to Gareth Barry for inviting me to his stag week in Las Vegas, even though I couldn't make it.

Prologue

He couldn't get to Sean McReynolds. But he sure could get to his son.

Sean McReynolds had spent his whole life killing Brits. Now the stupid bastards were saving his life: the Witness Protection Programme, they called it.

Well, it sure worked. Liam 'the Slaughterman' Dooley couldn't get anywhere near him.

But the bastard was responsible for the death of so many of his friends.

And he couldn't get near him.

But he could get to his son.

Danny McReynolds, the new George Best – 'Danny Boy' to all Ireland.

Star player with Man U.

Up there with Rooney and Ronaldo.

£100,000 a week.

Obscene...

'Danny Boy', the Irish wonder kid.

The new Georgy Best.

Bollocks.

He didn't even deserve to be mentioned in the same breath as our George.

It takes time to prove you're as good as George.

And Danny Boy didn't have it.

One

Villa Park, Birmingham.

Night game, an hour before kick-off.

It was sold out.

Manchester United v Aston Villa.

The ground was heaving. You could eat the atmosphere. The bars were packed. The beer was being drunk and spilled. The food sellers were doing a roaring trade and security was everywhere.

It was a big game.

The new pitch was green and lush. The four banks of spotlights in each corner illuminated the place in unprecedented light.

Liam 'the Slaughterman' walked through the jostling crowds. He had on his green overall with 'ELECTRICAL TECHNICIAN' lettered on the back and he carried his green canvas bag, also with the same logo. Hanging from his neck was a plastic ID card facing his chest.

Two security men were paying him attention.

He walked straight towards them and in his best Irish accent he said, 'Greetings, auld son… sure to be a fine auld game. How do you see it going?'

'Evening, Paddy,' greeted one of them.

'God bless you.'

They noted the logos.

'I can't see them getting past the Villa keeper tonight,' one of the guards said. 'The way he's been playing lately he could stop a bullet.' He laughed.

Dooley beamed a smile and laughed too. 'Sure, I suppose anything's possible.'

The second fuck-up spoke. 'What about Danny Boy? How do you see him?'

'I'm sure he'll get a shot in front of goal. Trust me on that.'

The first fuck-up spoke again. 'What's your job tonight, Paddy?'

Dooley sighed. 'Got to stand on the roof, all on me own, by one of the spotlights in case of failure. There's so much power being used...' He let it trail off. 'Well, you never know.'

'Good luck, Paddy,' said fuck-up no. 1.

'And yourself too, auld son,' said Dooley as he walked to the door that led to some concrete steps up to the gantry. 'It's locked, auld son. Would you be after trying to get me the sack?'

The two fuck-ups laughed.

'Sorry, Paddy!'

One of them opened the door.

Dooley flashed him a mischievous smile, saluted and started up to the roof.

'Nice guy.'

'Yeah, a real character.'

Two

Dooley gazed down from behind the spotlights. The view was spectacular. The crowds were massing to take their seats. The noise reminded Dooley of one of those wildlife programmes in an African game park. Hyenas, birds, gazelles, wild buffalo – all jostling for their bit of territory.

He liked it up here.

Alone.

Pitch black behind him.

Bright lights in front of him.

He knew from his early reconnaissance that day that he couldn't be seen. He'd mingled confidently with the army of workmen and blagged his way round the ground.

He just hoped that no one found the poor bastard that he'd knocked out, gagged, tied up and locked in a distant, out of the way cupboard.

Just for his worker's pass.

He untied the green canvas bag and removed the components for his sniper's rifle. He began to assemble the gun carefully, checking everything twice. Before he had left his hotel room he had meticulously cleaned and oiled every component. Finally he fitted the scope and the silencer to the long barrel.

He was ready.

He leaned back against the four foot high wall in the semi-dark and fished in his pocket. He pulled out his tin and tools and built a cigarette. He lit it with an old Zippo and took a deep drag.

He looked at his watch. Ten minutes till the game started.

The clock was ticking for Danny Boy.

The new George Best.

'Well, the two of yez can argue about it later,' he said to himself out loud and chuckled.

He could just see Sean McReynolds now sitting in front of the

TV with his Guinness waiting for Danny fucking wonder boy to strut his stuff.

For the last time. Dooley 'the Slaughterman' reached inside his overalls and pulled out a small hip flask. It contained Bushmills Irish whiskey. He removed the top and took a long draw.

'To yourself, Sean, you traitorous bastard. Enjoy the game.'

He laughed madly and took another swig.

Three

There was a deafening roar in the stadium that shook the spotlights.

This was it…

Liam Dooley sang a song he remembered from his childhood. Only he changed the words a bit.

He sucked on the smoke.

'Hold up your head, Liam Dooley. Hold up your head, don't cry. Hold up your head, Liam Dooley. Danny Boy's going to die!'

He'd rehearsed that in his head all day.

He laughed again to himself and flicked away the remainder of the cigarette.

He scrambled to his feet and looked over the wall.

The players were in position.

Danny fucking wonder boy was on the centre spot, his boot on the ball. He looked from left to right at the two players on either side of him.

The ref checked his watch. Put the whistle in his mouth.

He looked at the linesman.

He blew.

It had started.

Danny fucking wonder boy flicked the ball to the player on his right, then raced off towards the Villa goal at the far end of the pitch from Dooley.

Dooley sighed sadly.

The game would have to end in the first half.

Shame. But never mind.

The Slaughterman was enjoying the game.

It was end-to-end stuff.

Wonder Boy was dribbling and weaving around players like he thought he was George Best.

He hoped George was watching.

They'd have a lot to talk about after the game.

It was fifteen minutes gone.

Dooley reached for the sniper rifle. He positioned himself on the wall and took a look through the sights.

The cross hairs followed Danny Boy with every swerve he made.

It was an easy shot. Any decent sniper could make it.

Easy-peasy, for the best shot in the IRA.

The Villa keeper could stop a bullet!

'Well, I hope he doesn't get in the way,' Dooley muttered.

The winger crossed the ball to the feet of Danny Boy. He stopped it dead with perfection. He turned, swivelled, danced, and moved the ball from the mesmerised defender. Made a fucking eejit of the centre back, stopped ready to drill the ball past the keeper, who was crouched waiting, then took off again to everyone's surprise and ran behind the keeper to walk the ball into the net.

The crowd went mad.

Even the Villa fans clapped.

Danny Boy started charging around the pitch, punching the air.

The cross hairs moved to the middle of his back.

Dooley gently squeezed the trigger.

The rifle coughed.

A small puff of smoke emptied from the barrel.

Danny Boy seemed to trip and fall on his face.

The whole ground roared with laughter.

That was the funniest thing they ever saw.

Ha ha ha.

Teammates ran over to pick him up.

He wasn't moving.

Bodies fell to their knees all around him.

His red shirt was soaked – a darker red.

The funny thing was that his white name and number were also red.

You could have heard a pin drop in the ground now.

But nobody knew what was happening.

The officials moved in.

'Fucking hell! He's been shot.'

'He's dead.'

Four

Dooley burst through the door at the bottom of the steps.

The two fuck-ups turned, startled.

'Paddy!'

'What in the name of Jesus is going on?'

Fuck-up one said, 'No idea, Paddy.'

Fuck-up two said, 'They've abandoned the game.'

'Jesus, Mary and Joseph! What does that mean?'

'Total fucking chaos!' said fuck-up one.

'And me with me sick mother to attend to.'

'If I was you, Paddy, I'd get out of here fast, then,' said fuck-up no. 2.

'Sure, St Patrick himself couldn't get through that lot from here,' Dooley moaned. ' 'Tis me poor mother I'm worried about. She'll need changing soon.'

Fuck-up no. 1 raised both hands in the air and said, 'Calm down, calm down!' He called across the hall, 'Simon, Simon! Do us a favour, mate. Open that door for Paddy, will ya? His mom's sick and he needs to get out of 'ere.'

'No probs.'

'Go down them steps, turn left at the end of the building and you're in the staff car park. Walk across. You'll see the barrier. Then you're out the ground.'

Dooley thrust out his hand and shook with both men.

'God bless you both. Me sainted mother will remember you in her prayers.'

He moved quickly across the hall to the door. He thrust his hand to the third man. 'You too, auld son.'

The door slammed hard behind him.

He reached the barrier and a security man stepped out of his box.

'Top of the evening to ye!' called Paddy.

'Finished early?'

'They've abandoned the game.'
'I heard it on the radio… Know why?'
'Somebody said one of the players caught his death.'

Five

Costa del Sol, Andalucia
A farmhouse in the country

I'd stolen £20 million worth of drugs from some bad people and sold the lot for £5 million cash.

I'd ripped off an Irish thug called Liam O'Connor for 2 million.

They were mad at me. The drug barons sent hit men.

O'Connor sent ex-IRA.

The underworld on the Costa del Sol somehow got involved and murdered my best friend.

I tried, sentenced to death and hanged the one who killed my friend.

The others came for me one dark night at my farm.

With the help of my new best friend, Jesús Alcantara, an ex-ETA Special Forces soldier, we trapped and killed them all by the pool.

My next best friend, Sebastian Aparicio, a Spanish police motorcycle patrolman, had the bodies removed and cremated by his cousin who worked at the crematorium.

Peace at last...

Barbara was my latest girlfriend. She was twenty-two, seventeen years younger than me. She was beautiful, slim with long dark hair and an all-over tan.

We had a soft double lounger that we kept close to the pool. We lay on it that morning in the warm spring sunshine. The sky was clear blue Spanish. The scent of citrus drifted across the pool from the lemon and orange grove. A faint breeze brought a taste of the dry Spanish earth. A few birds sang happily.

Even though I say it myself, I'm fit, ex-Army, toned and in good shape. A deep all-over tan helps too.

My friends nicknamed me 'Magnum', as in Magnum PI. I

never argued with that, although I always thought I had the edge on looks.

I rolled over and very softly and gently kissed Barbara on the lips.

'Pina colada?'

'You bet.'

We never wore clothes around the farm. There was no need. We had no neighbours for miles. But we dressed immediately if we heard visitors.

Barbara always wore a top. My idea.

I had built my own bar by the pool. You could have opened it to the public.

I got up, extended my hand to Barbara.

'We'll drink in the shade.'

I pulled her up.

We took a few steps to the bar. Barbara sat on a stool, I went behind.

The clinking of ice, the pouring of drinks, a slice of pineapple.

I placed both drinks on the counter and took a bar stool next to Barbara.

We clinked glasses and drank.

'Jack...' Barbara started hesitantly.

'What is it?'

'When can we drive to the lake again?'

The lake...

I was diving in a huge lake in the mountains when I came across a crashed Learjet that had been lost for over twenty years.

It was full of gold ingots. It turned out that they were part of the proceeds from the famous Brink's-Mat bullion robbery.

Barbara had originally been a pupil at my dive school in England.

I had taken her to the plane and now she was bewitched with it. She was always wanting to go back and see it again.

'Any time you like.'

'You mean it?'

'Of course. Why not?'

She leaned over and gave me a huge pina colada kiss. I took a drink of mine, deliberately soaking my moustache. She kissed me passionately, draining the cocktail from my upper lip.

We put down the drinks and gently slipped off the stools into each other's arms.

We kissed again and then she said, 'That was the most fantastic day of my life, Jack. Swimming up to that plane and seeing all that gold was amazing. I'll never forget it.'

'We'll go back again soon,' I promised.

There were millions of pounds in gold in the hold of the plane and it was still there. I'd only taken a couple of ingots. I'd left the gold where it was because I didn't need it. The plane was far out in the water at the deepest location. Nobody was allowed to dive there so it was perfectly safe.

We took our drinks and sat on the edge of the lounger.

'It's so beautiful here, Jack. I can't believe how lucky I am.'

'No,' I said truthfully, 'it's me that's the lucky one. You've made me really happy.'

'You're so sweet, Jack,' she told me shyly. 'You know how much I love you, don't you?'

'Of course I do.'

We put our drinks on the floor and rolled back gently onto the sun bed. We kissed and petted and whispered words of love to each other. We gradually built up the passion as Barbara climbed on top of me. She took my manhood and slipped it into her with a groan.

I lay back in ecstasy, holding myself back, waiting for the right time when I thought Barbara was ready. Her climax was slowly building. I could feel it. Her hands pressed hard into my chest. Her face began to screw up. She bit her bottom lip. I felt it start so I relaxed and let go. And at exactly the same moment we cried out with pleasure and ecstasy.

We gradually slowed like a braking car. When we were done she lowered herself onto my chest and kissed me softly.

'That was fantastic, Jack,' she told me truthfully.

'Well, you know what I always say,' I grinned. 'If you can't be good, be great.'

By the way, the name's Jack.

Jack Reec.

Six

The sex had made us hungry. I lit the barbecue. I pulled a bottle of cold cava from the fridge and popped the cork. Two Waterford crystal glasses clinked in my hand as I placed them on the bar. I poured and we drank and I poured some more.

I hauled in a deep breath of the fresh, clean, pure Costa air. It was just past noon. The barbecue had stopped smoking and the coals were glowing red.

I held Barbara's hand.

We didn't need to speak.

It had all been said before.

This is the life.

I heard the chug of a slow motorbike in the distance.

Sebastian...

Unhurriedly, I put on shorts. Barbara put on a yellow bikini. Sebastian knew the drill. He always gave us time to dress.

He glided slowly into the yard, a light trail of farm dust showing his trail.

'*Buenas tardes.*'

'*Buenas tardes.*'

Sebastian was small and slim with a permanent built-in smile. He dismounted his motorcycle and removed his helmet and gloves.

He shook my hand warmly and kissed Barbara on both cheeks.

'A fabulously beautiful day again, señor,' he said by way of greeting.

'Always is, amigo,' I answered back. 'Can I offer you a drink?'

'*Gracias; cerveza.*'

I passed him a freezing San Miguel.

He wiped the neck and drank it in one.

'*Muchas.*'

'Another one?'

'*Sí, señor.*'

I gave him another one.

He just drank the top off that one.

'How is life today, señor?' he asked.

'I didn't think it could get any better,' I laughed. 'But now you're here.'

We all laughed.

Without asking I threw food on the barbecue.

Pre-seasoned peppered fillet steaks, minted lamb chops and for speed giant prawns in garlic.

Over the top on the prawns. But they got eaten.

Forking over the meat, I asked, 'How is the patrol today?'

He looked serious for a moment. Then very thoughtfully he chose his words. 'Amigo, today I have decided to give an amnesty to the speeding tourists. I have decided for one afternoon to show kindness and mercy!'

I eyed him with suspicion. 'You mean that you decided to come here to eat and get drunk?'

'Perhaps.'

That was the signal. I tossed him a pair of shorts and he went off to get changed.

We ate, partied and swam all afternoon.

We reminisced about old times. Told jokes – some good, some bad.

Then it was time to go.

Sebastian Aparicio changed back into a Spanish policeman. And not for the first time in my life, I helped him onto his bike.

'*Adios, amigo!*'

He rode off.

The dusk crept up; the night birds chirped.

The lights were on around the pool. Barbara lay reading a book.

I sat back in a lounger, a cigar in one hand, a brandy in the other.

The night smells had replaced the day smells. The same ones, but with a hint of dampness. Yet it was all so pure.

I thought about the past girls in my life.

Most of them dead.

Violent deaths…
I wondered what would happen to Barbara.

Seven

A safe house somewhere in Great Britain

Sean McReynolds was settling down in front of the television with a cool box full of Guinness and a freshly delivered pizza.

This was a big day. Danny Boy, the toast of all the land, the new George Best, was leading out Manchester United against Aston Villa at the magnificent Villa Park.

His son. Danny McReynolds.

Leading out Man U.

The thrill of it!

Shame about the two goons.

Special Branch?

Witness protection?

MI5?

MI6?

HM Secret Service?

Mickey Mouse?

Donald Duck?

Didn't know who they were.

Didn't give a fuck, either.

They were in the way.

That's all he knew.

'Give me some fucking space, will yez,' he grumbled pushing out his elbows.

'Take a chill pill, Paddy,' said goon no. 1.

'Jazus, save me from fuckin' eejits!'

Danny Boy started the game. He was playing well.

The two goons were enjoying it too. All three took pieces of pizza and cracked open cans.

'See my boy!' screamed McReynolds. 'What a player.'

Danny Boy scored.

Sean McReynolds roared like a speared grizzly bear.

He jumped to his feet, throwing the pizza at the ceiling and sending three cans of Guinness careering across the room, spraying foam like a fire extinguisher in every direction.

'For fuck's sake, you thick Irish cunt!' roared goon no. 2.

'What the fuck…'

'Did you see that, did you see that?'

'Yeah, we saw it.'

'Wasn't it great, wasn't it great?'

'Yeah, fucking great.'

'What a goal!'

'Yeah, yeah. Who's cleaning the mess up?'

'Fuck the mess! Hang on, what's going on?'

The television seemed as if it was on mute.

Then…

Then the commentator's voice came on – quiet and earnest. 'There seems to be something seriously wrong on the pitch. We have no definite information at the moment. There appears to have been a serious accident of some kind. But we can't tell you at this stage what it is. Excuse me a minute… it seems that the game is to be abandoned. Doctors and paramedics are on the scene treating Danny McReynolds, the Manchester United captain. We have just received information that the Air Ambulance is on the way and that the ground is being sealed. That's all I can tell you at this time, folks. So let's take a commercial break.

Sean McReynolds had gone berserk. The goons were trying to restrain him.

But it would take a straightjacket.

'A fucking commercial break! I want to know what's happened to my son!'

Goon no. 1 one grabbed a bottle of Irish whiskey and a tumbler. He poured three fingers.

'Sean, Sean, Sean, listen to me. Quiet down, have a drink. Stay calm. Drink this and I'll get a direct line to my superiors and we'll have all the answers in seconds. Turn off the TV.'

The goon put an arm around McReynolds. He actually felt sorry for the man.

It was his fucking son, after all.

Sean McReynolds sat down and drained the glass.

Goon no. 1 closed his phone. He poured three more fingers and passed it over.

'It'll help.'

'With what?'

'Drink some first.'

He did.

'Sean.'

'What?'

The goon poured three more fingers in two more tumblers. He passed one to the other goon.

They both downed them in one.

'Sean, your son is dead. He was shot in the back.'

'In the back?'

'Yes. I'm sorry.'

The goons had never seen such grief.

Eight

Liam 'the Slaughterman' Dooley strolled across Birmingham. He headed to a late night bar where he could blend in. He had removed his overalls and put them in the canvas bag with the gun.

He needed a drink.

The pub-bar, whatever it was, was close to the Birmingham wholesale market.

He wasn't called the Slaughterman just because of his skills as an assassin. He had in fact been a butcher and slaughterer in his youth. Just like his father before him.

Slaughtering animals was the perfect apprenticeship to slaughtering human beings. Wasn't it?

He sat in a corner with a pint of Guinness.

Well, this was an Irish bar.

If it was crap here, then he had no chance.

He sipped the Guinness.

It was all right.

Nothing like Dublin.

But, hey, he knew that anyway.

But it was all right.

It was going to be a long night. He wanted to avoid hotels. Too many questions... ID.

He had a plan.

He always had a plan.

He needed to get rid of the bag and the gun as best he could.

It was untraceable, of course, and he'd cleaned it meticulously.

But not turning up was better.

He knew there were giant skips in the wholesale market's tons of rubbish.

He also knew that the fruit and veg market worked almost all night, as did the fish, which was almost closing up by 7 a.m.

The meat got going about 4 a.m.

He aimed at entering the market at about 3 a.m.

He could have done with a doze. But he contented himself with a couple of pints.

To doze in a pub would cause instant attraction.

He kept himself to himself.

But shit, the time dragged.

The hands on the clock crawled around.

It was finally 2.50.

Thank God for that.

He walked through the main gates of the Birmingham wholesale markets precinct, Pershore Street, at 3 a.m. unchallenged.

He was in.

You could have been mistaken for thinking it was three o'clock in the afternoon.

Christ! Were these people untidy!

There was rotting fruit and veg strewn all over the backs of the pitches, in the roads and down the aisles.

The fish was the same.

Fish smelling, ice everywhere. White polystyrene boxes dumped all over the place. They obviously didn't have to clean it up themselves.

Too busy for Dooley.

Dooley crossed the rough, bumpy road dividing the fish and poultry from the meat.

The meat side was like a ghost town by comparison.

Discarded chicken boxes, mostly. He walked through the central passage to the back.

This was the end.

The market's perimeter wall.

Deserted.

Perfect.

He stashed the bag.

And went for a walk.

He found what he wanted: abandoned empty brown potato bags. Fruit boxes stuffed with empty cardboard and brown paper. Banana boxes stuffed with debris.

Perfect camouflage.

Bit by bit he collected what he wanted. And bit by bit he took it to his deserted area behind Meals Direct, who didn't start till late.

When he had enough he got to work completely alone.

He broke down the gun into as many components as he could.

He put one little bit into each piece of camouflage.

He cut up the bag.

He cut up the overalls.

And by six in the morning every skip in the market had one bit.

A jigsaw is easy when every piece is in the box.

But when there's one piece in every corner of the country...

Not so easy.

Nine

Sean McReynolds was exhausted. He sat in front of the TV with a tumbler of Bushmills.

It was almost 10 p.m.

He was waiting for the ITV News. Not that they would know any more than he did. Probably less.

The familiar theme tune played.

'Good evening, this is ITV *News at Ten* with Trevor McDonald.'

Sean McReynolds leaned back into the cushion on the sofa.

'The mystery deepens after the apparent assassination of Manchester United captain Danny McReynolds. Police have issued a statement saying that a contract worker, an electrician, was on the roof at the time in the approximate vicinity of the spot from which the shot was fired. Police are appealing for him to come forward as he may have some vital information.'

'Fucking fat chance of that!' McReynolds roared furiously.

'Meanwhile,' continued Trevor McDonald, 'it has been revealed that after a thorough search of the ground police found a man tied up in a cupboard. He was apparently an outside worker who had been robbed of his day ground pass. This has cast suspicion that the worker on the roof, may not have been genuine. In fact he may even be the assassin. So let's cross to Howard Johnson at Villa Park...'

There was a split-second delay, then:

'Yes, Trevor, there does seem a lot of confusion here. One of the huge questions being asked is how could a sniper smuggle a rifle into Villa Park and get onto the roof? The even bigger question is how, after killing Danny McReynolds, he could evaporate into thin air with the gun. Yes, Trevor, a lot of questions to be answered. This is Howard Johnson for *ITN News* handing you back to the studios.'

McReynolds was raging like a mad dog. The goons tried to calm him.

'Sean, Sean, stay calm. There's more, listen.'

Trevor McDonald took up the story again. 'Police, after interviewing the only three people to see the "electrician", have built up a description and put together an artist's impression of the man.'

A face drawn in black and white filled the screen.

Sean McReynolds dropped his tumbler. The contents fell into his lap.

He was staring at the face of Liam 'the Slaughterman' Dooley.

Ten

At five minutes past six Liam Dooley was standing at the bus stop by the Kerry Man pub, Digbeth.

He was waiting for the 900. It was a frequent service, every twenty minutes, so he hadn't to wait very long. The empty bus stopped. He stepped on, paid the disinterested driver and went upstairs.

He could have taken a taxi, but taxi drivers talk too much. Anyway the bus was just as quick. And no questions.

The bus would drop him outside the departures at Birmingham International. It was only half an hour or so from the city centre, giving him lots of time to catch the 8 a.m. Aer Lingus flight to Dublin.

He had on him every possible piece of documentation he would need to fly worldwide if necessary. Passport, ID, driving licence, credit cards, even a birth certificate.

In the name of Jack Flynn.

Of course.

Eleven

Sean McReynolds jumped out of his seat.

'That's Liam Dooley – the Slaughterman! I'd know him any-where. He's the biggest murdering bastard that ever walked Ireland!'

'That's rich coming from you,' swiped one of the goons cynically.

McReynolds lunged at him. The second goon grabbed him. The first one drew a Glock. 'Steady,' he warned. 'Just remember, the only circumstances I'm allowed to kill you are in self-defence.'

'That's Liam Dooley.'

'Of course it is, we know.'

'So what are you doing about it?'

'Plenty.'

'Like what?'

'Leave that to us.'

'I want to talk to the boys.'

'All in good time, Sean.'

'Huh!'

'Leave it to us, Sean. Leave it to us.'

He handed the Irishman a replacement drink.

Twelve

A meeting of a cell of the IRA somewhere in Ireland

There were six in all at the council.

Plus Dooley.

Two speakers.

Four listeners.

Vincent McGuire and Joe Cahill were the speakers. The four also-rans would not speak unless requested.

They were rarely requested.

The six were seated at a table in the back room of a pub. Each man had a pint of Guinness in varying degrees of height. In the middle of the table was a bottle of Bushmills and a dozen or so tumblers.

Liam Dooley 'the Slaughterman' leaned against the side wall building a cigarette.

'Liam, auld son, 'tis good to see you again,' greeted Vincent McGuire, opening the proceedings.

'A fine sight you all are indeed,' beamed Dooley.

He finished rolling his fag and lit it up with the Zippo. The whole room waited silently while he had a smoke. As he relaxed, everyone also relaxed.

'Will yez take a drink, Liam?' asked Joe Cahill, the second of the speakers.

'To be sure I will, Joey Boy. Bushmills – mother's milk.'

There were smiles and a light buzz of laughter as one of the foot soldiers poured and passed a glass.

Everybody waited, reverently it seemed, until Dooley had finished his roll-up and had a drink.

'So now that you've finished your personal business,' began Vincent McGuire, 'can we get to the real business?'

Dooley raised a hand.

'Correction! I'm not finished, I've just left a deposit on the finished job. The job will never be finished until I see McReynolds drowning in his own blood.'

McGuire sighed deeply. 'And to be sure, I don't doubt that for a minute.'

'Don't.'

Dooley started building another cigarette. 'So this Jack Reec. Fill me in.'

'Patsy Cronin,' began McGuire. 'He was sent to take out Reec. He got killed in the field.'

Dooley licked his fag paper. 'No mean feat.'

'Yes, I know,' McGuire begrudgingly agreed.

Dooley lit up again. 'And?'

'Liam O'Connor, Finbarr O'Shaughnessy, Micky Yallop and Patsy's brother, Michael Cronin, went after him.

'And?'

'They disappeared. We never heard from them again.'

Dooley took a drink, sucked his roll-up and burst into peals of laughter.

The six men at the table waited until he had satisfied his amusement.

'So you're telling me that five of the hardest men in all Ireland were taken out by Reec?'

'Plus two blacks. Yardie drug dealers.'

Dooley howled with laughter. He held out his glass. 'Fill me up!' He sucked on the fag. 'So what are you offering me? 20 million euros?'

Thirteen

Trevor McDonald was talking to Sean McReynolds.

Well, that's how he saw it anyway.

Trevor said, 'Latest news on the murder of Manchester United captain Danny McReynolds indicates that the police have no new leads. Apart from a description of a suspect, there is nothing else. There is no trace of the murder weapon and there was no sighting of the witness. It seems he has fled the country or gone to ground. The police are continuing with their enquiries.'

'That's bollocks!' shouted McReynolds. 'I told you who it is – it's Liam Dooley!'

'Sean, Sean,' reasoned goon no. 1. 'Our people are dealing with it. Listen to me. You don't think we're going to share information with the local plod, do you? You must know they're a load of wankers and will charge in feet first and tell the whole world they're looking for Liam Dooley. And have you seen him?'

'Yeah, I suppose so.'

'So what we want to do is just keep low, send in the specialists and take him out quietly. It doesn't bring back Danny Boy, but at least you've evened the score.'

'Give me a drink, auld son, will ya.'

A goon passed him a large tumbler.

'When will I know it's done?'

'The moment we hear.'

'Thanks.'

He drank some whiskey and began to sob quietly.

The goons left him to his grief and backed into the kitchen.

The one goon said to the other, 'What's the real score?'

The other replied, 'Top brass don't give a fuck about Sean McReynolds or his son. Liam Dooley is a real pro. He hasn't left a clue. There's not a fart in a hurricane's chance of bringing him to court, and we certainly aren't sacrificing good men to take him out.'

'It's finished.'

'And off the record.'

'Yes?'

'I hope he gets to McReynolds eventually. He's nothing but a murdering IRA bastard. And you want to know something else?'

'What?'

'He's nothing but a traitor to his own cause.'

'And I hate that.'

'It's over.'

Fourteen

We had planned a barbecue for the night Jesús Alcantara and Sebastian Aparicio were coming. Barbara and myself had been preparing food all day.

We had laid a table extravagantly with the finest tablecloth from one of the best mills in Spain. The glasses were Waterford crystal from Ireland. The dinner service was Spanish from one of the best stores in Malaga. Two silver ice buckets stood at either end of the table, half full of ice and water.

One contained cava, the other a bottle of Chilean Chenin Blanc. A bottle of red breathed on the table. Napkins with silver rings were set at each place. Flowers from the garden decorated the table along with a bowl of fresh fruit.

Barbara was dressed in a pink flowing evening dress with dainty pink shoes to match. She wore her hair up.

She looked sensational.

I was wearing white linen trousers, a short-sleeved open-necked shirt and comfortable cream canvas shoes.

I too looked sensational.

The evening was warm, but not sticky. The sun was slowly going down and the evening was settling in. A few birds called to each other across the garden.

'Thanks, Barb,' I said. 'You've done a fantastic job.'

'*De nada*. You're welcome.'

'I mean it. Thanks. I really appreciate it.'

'Don't be so daft. Do me a drink.'

'What would you like?'

'I want you to take me to heaven. Just like Jesús does.'

Of course I knew then exactly what she wanted: a Harvey Wallbanger.

Jesús Alcantara was full of bullshit. The first time he had met Barbara, he steered her away from me towards the bar.

'Señorita,' I heard him say, 'I'm renowned through the whole of Andalucia for my amazing Harvey Wallbanger. Let me take you to heaven.'

I smiled to myself as I fixed two drinks in tall glasses. Ice first, vodka second, Galliano and fresh orange juice. Straight from the garden. I decorated it with fancy straws and a slice of orange.

We sat at a small table by the pool. The smell of charcoal passed beneath my nose.

'I'm really excited about tonight,' enthused Barbara. 'I haven't seen Jesús for ages.'

'Yeah, well, just don't get too excited,' I teased. 'I wouldn't trust him an inch where you're concerned. The man has no honour.'

'That's not true,' she snapped. 'Jesús is a perfect gentleman.'

'A bullshitting bastard, more like.'

'You better not mean that, Jack.'

'I don't.'

'Because if you do…'

'I don't.'

'Well, you'd better not.'

'I said I don't.'

I started laughing.

'You're a pig, Jack.'

'Yes I know. Funny though.'

I laughed some more and, trying not to, she just couldn't help joining in.

I saw the headlights before I heard the honk of the horn. A silver Mercedes SLK 200 cruised to a stop in the yard. The hood was down and I could see Jesús and Sebastian opening the doors to get out.

'*Buenas tardes.*'

'*Hola!*'

'*Buenas tardes.*

'*Hola!*'

We got through all the greetings.

'A drink, amigos?' I asked.

'*Una cerveza,*' replied Jesús.

'I also, señor,' said Sebastian. 'Señorita Barbara, may I compliment you on your beautiful appearance. You look truly breathtaking.'

Jesús Alcantara stepped forward. He snapped his heels, took her hand and kissed it.

'How can I follow that, señorita? Except to say how whole-heartedly I agree.'

I grinned broadly. 'I think the cows must be moving in from the fields. I can smell something really…'

Jesús Alcantara stopped me. 'You threaten my honour, señor, with such disrespectful talk.'

'Shut up,' I said. 'Let's start the party.'

To the sound of laughter we started to eat. Cold meat, fish and salad to start. It was every man for himself. We stood around talking and drinking.

As it began to get dark I put the lights on. The barbecue hissed as I forked on eight boneless chicken thighs in Valencian garlic.

The smell…

Barbara, Jesús and Sebastian sat at the table as I served the first course and sat with them. We each chose our own wine and talked around the table.

'Amigo.' Jesús was addressing me. 'Is it possible that you can do me a great favour?'

'Obviously, if it's within my power,' I replied. 'Consider it done. What is it?'

'A very special friend of mine, José Miguel Gallega,' Jesús began. 'His yacht will be arriving in Puerto Banus sometime in the week. His wife, María Luisa Gallega, will be on board. She will be here for probably a week. He has asked me if I can look out for her and perhaps show her around.'

'So what's the problem?' I asked.

'I am going to be in the Basque region for a few days and will not be here to greet her. I wondered if you could possibly meet her at the port.'

'Of course, amigo. How could that be a problem?'

'*Gracias*, Jack.'

'No problem. Anything more I should know?'

'She's travelling with a friend, Sonia Carabantes.'

We ate, drank and danced until the early hours of the morning. A small orange glow began to shine on the horizon as the SLK 200 cruised easily away from the farm.

Fifteen

Dooley was on his third roll-up and second Bushmills.

'This Reec seems like no pushover to me,' he declared.

'And me looking forward to quiet retirement and all that. He's got to have backup. What do you know?'

'Our intelligence…'

'Fuck me, that's a big word for the likes of you! Go on.'

A little irritably, Vincent McGuire continued. 'He appears to work with a man called Jesús Alcantara, ex Special Forces, now working for ETA. He is also linked to the Spanish Police Force through his association with an officer called Sebastian Aparicio. We believe through these men Reec has access to unlimited arms and manpower.'

Dooley could not help laughing.

'What's so funny, Liam?' asked Joe Cahill.

'Youse lot, sitting there on yer arses expecting me to take on the Spanish Police Force, ETA and Jack Reec all on me own! Yer a load of fucking gobshites.'

'Watch your fucking mouth, Dooley!' snapped McGuire. 'Just remember who you're talking to.'

Dooley smashed his glass into the pile on the table. They scattered and broke everywhere.

There was a fearful and startled look on every man's face in the room.

In a flash there was a Glock handgun in Dooley's hand.

Dooley spat, 'I'll drill every man jack of yer if youse ever speak to me that way again.'

'I didn't mean it like that,' stumbled McGuire.

'How did you fuckin' mean it, then?'

'Well, I mean, this is the council.'

'And?'

'Well you should show a little respect.'

'For the council? The war's fucking *over*! You're just playing soldiers.'

There was an uneasy silence as Dooley put the gun back inside his jacket.

'I seem to have dropped my drink.'

One of the foot soldiers hurriedly fixed a fresh one.

Dooley drank.

'So where were we?' He relit the fag that had gone out. 'Reec. What exactly has he done?'

'He killed five of our best men.'

'I mean, what has he done against the cause? If there is a cause any more.'

'He murdered five of our best men. Friends of ours,' piped up Joe Cahill.

'Murdered, huh? That's a strong word. They went after him to kill him. What did you think he was going to do? Greet them at the airport?'

'Liam,' sighed Vincent McGuire, 'what's going down here?'

'I'll get straight to the point here, auld son. My job was chief enforcer for the IRA. Redundant. The odd job crops up when someone takes the piss and steps out of line. I work for the cause. I'm not a hit man for hire. What's the deal? What are you offering me?'

'One million euros.'

'Hmm.'

'It's a lot of money, Liam.'

'It's not a lot of money to a dead man.'

Sixteen

Puerto Banus in my opinion is a shithole.

A wanker's paradise, frequented by tossers so far up their own arse that they can't see their heads.

So it was a great relief to me when I found out that María Luisa Gallega had diverted her yacht to Puerto Duquesa, thirteen kilometres west of Estepona.

Estepona is called 'the last paradise' – an exaggeration maybe, but you can see their point.

Puerto Duquesa, like Puerto Estepona, is a place to stroll around, sit at an outdoor café and absorb the atmosphere. Just beyond it on the shore is Castillo de Sabinillas, built in the seventeenth century to protect the coast from Berber pirates. A bit further on lies Cadiz province and its many attractions, including the exclusive urbanisation of Sotogrande and the sparkling new Puerto Sotogrande.

I had washed and hoovered the Jaguar XK8 convertible and cruised over to the port and was now sitting outside at a café waiting for my phone to ring.

It was a beautiful day, as always. I eased back in my chair and soaked in the beauty of the port through the crystal clarity of my Ray-Ban sunglasses.

People sat on their boats, cleaned their boats, fished from their boats and drank on their boats.

Tourists and sightseers strolled hand in hand, stopping occasionally to watch something unfold. Gulls hovered and swooped, squawking continuously.

I knew that the yacht and María Luisa Gallega had berthed and that she and Sonia Carabantes were meeting me at the café with overnight bags.

They were staying at the farm that night.

Barbara was taking care of the food and everything.

Good old Barb!

My phone rang. They were on their way. I looked up. I could see two fabulously elegant and beautiful Spanish women coming towards the café.

It had to be them.

It was.

We introduced ourselves.

They had a glass of wine, then I took their bags and showed them to the car.

They looked impressed.

We sped along to the farm at way over the speed limit.

I heard the siren as the police motorcyclist pulled me over.

Sebastian Aparicio removed his sunglasses and helmet.

'*Hola, amigo.*'

'*Hola.*'

I turned to the ladies in the back. 'Señoras, this is my very best friend, Sebastian Aparicio.'

I introduced them to Sebastian.

'My great pleasure to meet you both,' he beamed.

'Sebastian, the señoras are staying at the farm tonight. Do you think you could possibly call round? Otherwise I will be hopelessly outnumbered.'

'The best fighting bull in Andalucia could not keep me away, señor. Until tonight.'

And so it was.

An amazing night.

Amazing company.

And an amazing hangover.

Seventeen

Dooley decided to take the job. It would be his last hit. One million euros plus expenses. He wanted two good men to take with him, to even the odds. But he would have to pay for them out of his share.

He figured 50,000 euros each.

Good pay for a foot soldier.

He knew the men he wanted. Kevin Goulding – 'KG' to his friends.

He was cool, calm and reliable. And he would do as he was told.

Johnny McGouldrick, or Mr McGoo, as he was known.

McGoo was a loose cannon.

Radged in the head, someone once said.

He was really a drunken womaniser. A bit of a crazy.

But he was good to have around if there was something crazy to do. And you didn't want to do it yourself.

First to go in.

Last to come out.

Dooley set off to find them.

The Spotted Dog was a backstreet pub in Dublin favoured by a lot of 'The Boys'.

Dooley pushed through the door. There were greetings from everybody. They all knew Dooley: top man. Hero to all Ireland.

He grinned broadly and raised both arms in the air.

'God bless Ireland!'

There was a loud cheer.

The jukebox burst to life with the Pogues belting out 'Dirty Old Town'.

Feet banged on the wooden floor and glasses banged on tables. There was no place like Dublin.

There was a smoking ban in Ireland, but you wouldn't have thought so in the Spotted Dog. The air was a blue haze.

Nobody had ever tried to enforce the law; not here.

Rather strange.

Dooley forced his way to the bar.

The pretty girl behind it asked, 'What is it you'll be having, Liam? A large Bushmills while the Guinness is pouring?'

Dooley said with a glint in his eye, 'And afterwards maybe a sniff of the barmaid's apron.'

'Dream on, Dooley!' she laughed, passing the Bushmills and simultaneously starting the Guinness.

'KG and McGoo. Seen 'em?'

' 'Tis yer lucky day, if it's them scallywags yer after.'

'How so?'

'KG's cheating everybody's money off them in the back room, and Mr McGoo is probably under the table up Annie's skirt in the far corner.'

Dooley chuckled.

He downed the Bushmills just as the perfect pint was set down in front of him. He passed over the money.

'Keep the change, Andrea.'

'Thanks, Liam.'

'You're welcome.'

Dooley crossed the room to Johnny McGouldrick's table. He hadn't got his head up Annie's skirt but he was all over her. He was laughing loudly.

Annie was an old friend of Dooley's, sort of.

McGoo got to his feet, nearly knocking over the table and glasses.

'Jesus, Mary and Joseph! Liam Dooley. Annie…'

'I know the scut,' she spat.

Dooley acknowledged her.

'Annie.'

He spoke to McGoo. 'A word, auld son.'

Dooley crossed to the door to the back room. He opened it and saw Kevin Goulding in a corner playing cards. KG saw him.

He showed his cards. The game was over. He picked up the money and met Dooley halfway into the room.

'Kevin.'

'Liam.'

'A word if you can, auld son.'

Eighteen

The hiring was done.

The next few days were spent planning and organising. A Volvo estate was adapted with a hidden compartment in the floor to carry the guns. Food, drink, clothes, blankets were loaded into the back. Everything they thought they would need.

They took the ferry to England, the Tunnel to France, and now here they were crossing the border into Spain in a remote region where no one would ever know that they were there.

Spain.

They drove a few miles then stopped the car and got out.

The warm breeze hit them like a desert wind. It was just coming up to noon. They stretched and wandered around, surveying the terrain.

It was mountainous, with scrub and pine trees dotted everywhere. There was a vast landscape of dry, brown vegetation scorched by the Mediterranean sun.

Liam Dooley and Kevin Goulding lit up fags from a tin that they had built earlier. Johnny McGouldrick leaned into the back of the Volvo and pulled a half-litre bottle of beer from the cool box. He unscrewed the top and took a long swig.

'Startin' early, aren't we?' commented Dooley.

'You're assuming I stopped,' replied McGoo, laughing loudly at his own joke.

Goulding grinned. He liked McGoo. It was good to have him along.

Dooley said, 'John, you're supposed to be sharing the driving with Kevin, don't forget.'

'No problem, auld son,' said McGoo. 'There's nothing to hit around here for a hundred miles.'

'Just the same,' butted in Goulding, 'I'd feel safer doing it myself.'

'Sure you would!' laughed McGoo. 'And I'll respect yer wishes.' He had another slug.

'Where we headin' now?' asked Goulding.

Dooley had his map out.

'We're going to pick up the coast and head south. Malaga, Torremolinos then Fuengirola. There's a small one-horse town a few miles from here. We'll stop for a rest and a drink.'

'Sound by me,' grinned McGoo.

It sure was a one-horse town. Just a farmers' town. There were a couple of hundred homes, a few shops, a restaurant and a bar.

Goulding pulled up outside the bar, a cloud of dust blowing over the car. They all climbed out and had a stretch. Dooley led the way in.

Inside there were four leathery-faced locals with a drink and smoke. The barman was polishing a glass and seemed totally disinterested.

'*Hola, amigo*,' he mumbled.

He looked about a hundred.

He moved like he was 120.

Dooley announced, 'Three beers. Big beers.' Then, with a wave of his arms, he added, 'And drinks for everyone.'

Somebody must have understood. There was a rumble of approval from the 500-year-old crowd of four.

The barman began to move. Slowly.

'In yer own time, auld son,' said Dooley.

The Irishmen smiled at each other.

'Things is slow in Ireland,' chuckled Goulding, 'But this is taking the piss.'

They all lit up.

And waited.

The barman served all the locals first.

Dooley paid as they eventually got three large beers. They took them to a table across the room and sat down. They drank quietly for a few minutes while they cooled down.

Eventually Mr McGoo spoke. 'Have we got a plan, Liam? Or are we just making it up as we go along?'

Dooley gazed into his glass as if the answer lay in the bottom of it. He looked serious and thoughtful. KG and McGoo sat expectantly for his words of great wisdom.

Eventually he spoke.

'To be perfectly honest, boys, from the moment I decided to take the job I've tried to plan everything down to the last detail.'

'And?'

'I haven't got a fucking clue.'

All three roared heartily with laughter. Dooley called to the barman.

After three more beers and another round for the living dead, they vacated the premises.

They all agreed they'd never had so much fun!

They reached the coast and eventually bypassed Malaga and Torremolinos. They followed the signs for Fuengirola.

As with other places along the coast, there is a romantic tradition that Fuengirola was once a pretty fishing village where people lived an undisturbed life, and that all that has been ruined by tourist development. It is truer to say that before the tourist boom there was a poor, tatty village on an unwanted coast where people eked out a miserable life.

It is people with money in their pockets, normally foreigners and writers, who wistfully recall a scene and life they did not endure. You would be hard pressed to find a local person who wanted to return to the bad old days.

As with the other coastal towns, there is not much in the way of memorable sights. But there are some pleasant places to pass the time away. The Plaza de la Constitutión is dominated by the main church and surrounding bars have seating outdoors. Some nearby streets retain vestiges of their past. A few, like Calles Cruza and Moncayo, have been pedestrianised, and it is pleasant to have a meal at outdoor tables and watch the world go by.

The Irishmen were tired.

The first hotel they saw was Stella Maris, on Paseo Maritimo; an old favourite which commands a good position on the promenade in a residential area. It is close to the beach and ten minutes from the town centre. It has a swimming pool, horse riding, golf and tennis.

They took three rooms.

Nineteen

The three Irishmen met in the dining room for breakfast. It was self-service, so they helped themselves.

Kevin Goulding looked thoughtful. 'What's the state of play, then, Liam?'

'I reckon we should take a few days out and get together some sort of a plan. This Reec is no pushover. He's taken out the very best so we need to treat him with respect.'

The other two mumbled their agreement.

McGouldrick chewed on something and said, 'We have surprise. I'm sure nobody knows we're here. That's a real big advantage.'

'Too right it is,' chipped in Goulding. 'We got no rush. We just have to get things right. You figurin' a long-distance shot?'

'Ain't figurin' anything at the moment,' said Dooley, 'except figurin' not to get killed. Reec is a pro. *And* he's got backup. Good backup. But he ain't expectin' us.'

McGouldrick wanted to talk. When he was sober he made good sense. You had to get in quick. 'We know that he lives on an isolated farm. Right? So that has to be good for us. We can stake it out for a few days and get the routine of the place. Then, at the right time, Liam can make his shot and, like a mouse in the bog, we disappear.'

The other two mumbled their approval.

It didn't seem half bad.

Twenty

The day after the party I took the two señoras back to Puerto Duquesa.

It was Thursday. They were spending Friday on the boat. On Saturday, Jesús Alcantara would return from his trip. So it was fixed for a big party at the farm.

María Luisa Gallega was a rich and powerful woman. Her husband, José Miguel Gallega, was one of the richest men in Spain. He reared, among other things, the finest fighting bulls in Spain. He was preparing to run for local office.

Everyone who was anyone would want to be there.

Sonia Carabantes was organising the guest list. I had called in outside caterers. It was too big a job for me.

A four-piece Spanish band would provide the music, and four flamenco dancers would be the entertainment.

As a precaution, I hired a security firm, run by an ex-para that had a good name.

Billy Birmingham was the boss man's name, and after he realised the nature and the importance of the job, he decided to run the night himself – with three other men. His best.

Not cheap!

Barbara was coordinator.

Various vans and cars came and went, and a marquee rose up in the garden. A bar was set up inside it and stocked with everything. Two local Spanish barmen were hired to run it. It was their day off, so it earned them some extra cash.

And it wasn't a bad job either.

By Saturday afternoon everything was all but completed.

I drove to Puerto Duquesa and collected María Luisa Gallega and Sonia Carabantes.

Twenty-one

Liam Dooley and Kevin Goulding sat under an umbrella by the pool at the Stella Maris. Dooley was smoking a cheap Spanish cigar. Goulding stuck to his roll-up. They both drank pints of local lager.

Mr McGoo was sat at the pool bar with two women of about thirty-five in bikinis. They seemed to be having a great time.

The women were from Newcastle. Both married, but on a girls' holiday. McGouldrick was mesmerising them with his Irish charm and tales of the 'old country'.

Carole and Rita were here for a good time. And hell, so was McGoo... There was a bottle of cava in ice on the bar. Carole and Rita were drinking vodka and tonic to wash it down. Mr McGoo had a Guinness from a can and an Irish whiskey chaser.

They howled with laughter, McGoo kissing first one then the other.

Across the pool, Goulding chuckled. He really did like Johnny McGouldrick.

'Fancy a bet for a bit of fun?' asked Dooley.

'Sure, why not.'

'Which one do you think he'll end up with?'

'Both of them, of course.'

'You don't say!'

'To be sure, to be sure.'

McGoo ordered more drinks and the laughter got louder. He now had one hand placed firmly on each arse.

Then an arm around each waist.

Then a tit in each hand.

He seemed quite comfortable.

'Now, would one of you beautiful ladies pour some whiskey down me throat? I'm kind of occupied, as you can see.'

Squealing with laughter, Rita put the glass to his mouth and he drank it.

' 'Tis two fine Northern lasses that you are.' He laughed. 'And I have to sympathise with the dilemma you find yourselves in...'

'And what would that be, Paddy?' asked Carole, laughing.

'Sure, you must be wondering which of yez I'm taking to me bed!'

'Who said you're taking any of us?' put in Rita.

'Sure, God love yer, you both know the truth of it! And I'm not a man to cause trouble between friends. I'll make it easy for us. I've no favourite. Let's get a couple of bottles and head to my mattress for a bit of good old Irish fun!'

'Yeah!' they both cried. 'Some good old Irish fun.'

McGouldrick ordered two fresh bottles of cava and glasses. The girls carried the glasses and ice bucket, while McGoo carried the two bottles, with one arm wrapped around each girl's shoulder.

They walked unsteadily into the hotel.

Goulding and Dooley were chuckling across the pool.

'He's an awful cunt,' laughed Dooley.

'Well, to be honest,' confessed Goulding, 'at this present time I wouldn't mind being a cunt like McGoo.'

'I'd say that's the last we'll see of him today,' commented Dooley. He looked at his watch. It was 5 p.m. on a Saturday evening. 'I don't know about you, but I'm starting to get itchy feet. How do you feel about taking a ride over to Reec's farm and doing a little reconnoitre?'

'To be honest, that sounds good to me. The boredom seems to be setting in.'

'It'll pass a few hours,' Dooley said, 'then we can come back, have some food and a good drink.

'I think you've talked me into it, auld son.'

Twenty-two

Dooley and Goulding were fascinated. With binoculars they watched from a safe distance.

That was a real fucking hooley they were having. There were fancy sports cars, luxurious saloons, a couple of stretches and at least a dozen chauffeur-driven limos.

A few guys were walking around with chains around their necks, like they were lord mayors or something.

What was going on?

They looked at each other and just shrugged.

Good job they'd brought some cobs from the bar.

There was plenty of booze still in the car. They had some and watched.

It was early dusk. Most people had arrived.

Jack, Sebastian and Jesús were talking. Jesús Alcantara said to Jack, 'Jack, how can I ever thank you for this? I could never have afforded such a banquet. Not in a million years.'

'You saved my life, you fought at my side. So what is this small gesture in comparison?'

'Amigo…'

'Quiet. I'll hear no more.'

Sebastian Aparicio laughed. 'My Chief of Police keeps staring at me. He cannot believe that I am here.'

'Have fun, relax,' I told him.

'Of course, señor.'

There was a buzz of conversation around the farm. People moved from one to another. María Luisa Gallega and Sonia Carabantes, as the main event, mingled among the guests.

Dripping in diamonds and modelling the most expensive evening dresses you could imagine, they looked every inch the Spanish aristocrats.

Billy Birmingham and his three security men kept a discreet distance, but were always finely alert. Keeping an eye on everything.

Not that there could possibly be anyone who was likely to cause any trouble.

At what seemed a prearranged signal, the guitars of the band began belting out Spanish songs.

The barmen in the marquee were kept constantly busy, but as they soon realised, as it was a free bar, there were no tips.

Caramba!

Still, perhaps they would get a collection. You never could tell.

Next on, the flamenco dancers, shoes banging, castanets rattling, dresses swishing. *Fantástico.*

'I tell yer what, auld son,' laughed Goulding. 'He can organise a party at my place any time.'

'Yer've gotta hand it to him. *What the fuck…*'

In an instant the whole party turned to panic, fear and chaos.

Automatic gunfire.

Dooley and Goulding stared down at the crowd through their glasses.

There were six men, all in black with balaclavas. They were all armed with MAK 10 machine pistols. This gun, capable of firing twenty rounds per second, was nicknamed the Big Mac. It was a seriously deadly weapon.

'Nobody move!' screamed the apparent leader.

He let off a short burst into the air.

Everybody stood rock still, including the security.

Jack, Sebastian and Jesús exchanged glances. They were unarmed. What could they do?

'My Smith & Wesson is in the house,' Jack whispered to Jesús Alcantara.

'And best leave it there, señor. It is no match for a MAK 10.'

'We can't do nothing.'

'On this occasion, to do nothing is better than to do something. Believe me.'

'The first person that moves gets cut in half,' the leader threatened. 'Now, there's no reason for anyone to get hurt. Just listen to what I have to say. This is not political. It's just about money – plain and simple. Now, the ransom will be well within the pocket of the payer. It's only money. Nobody needs to get hurt. So stay calm.

He pointed the gun at María Luisa Gallega and Sonia Carabantes. 'Señoras, please step this way.'

They hesitated.

'*Now.*'

Hesitantly and fearfully, they left the safety of the crowd and stood by the gunman.

'We're taking these ladies with us. They will be well cared for and treated like the noble ladies that they are. You will receive our terms in due course and we expect you to accept them. For the ladies' sake, of course.'

I felt obliged to speak.

'I don't know who you are but you are making a big mistake. These people are guests in my home. I can't let you get away with this.'

'Good luck.'

It might have been bravery or foolishness, or maybe he thought he had an opportunity, but Billy Birmingham went for the gun inside his jacket.

A lethal burst from the Big Mac propelled him backwards into a table of drinks and food. Blood spurted from several holes in his body as the table and its contents shattered and disintegrated.

Billy Birmingham lay dead in a grotesque heap.

'That could so easily have been avoided,' said the leader. 'It was totally futile. Just a complete waste.'

He spoke to one of the other men, none of whom had said a word. 'Put the ladies in the car.'

He ushered them away into the dark where obviously there was a car waiting.

'You know what to do,' he said.

Two of the men in black broke away and, starting with the nearest car and working to the farthest, they shot out the tyres on every vehicle on the farm. Then they were off.

Nobody was following.

Absolutely no one, they thought.

But they were wrong.

Earnestly, Dooley said, 'Follow 'em, Kevin. No lights, don't lose them. I smell a real big cake on the plate here.'

'Sure thing, auld son.'

Twenty-three

For possibly the first time in my life I felt helpless. We could not give chase as we had no serviceable cars. Anyway, it was too late. There was nobody to follow. They were gone.

Oscar De la Hoya, Sebastian's boss, had taken charge. He had called the Policía Nacional, Spain's national police. It is they who are responsible for law and order and internal security.

They arrived, sirens blasting, in three cars. They ordered that nobody should leave. Billy Birmingham was covered with a blanket. Most of the guests were in shock.

Ambulances arrived. The crews began treating people and comforting them.

'How could this happen?' I asked nobody in particular.

'For me, amigo, this is a personal disaster,' said Jesús Alcantara despairingly. 'The señoras were under my protection. I have let them down. How can I tell my friend?'

'It wasn't your fault.' I tried to comfort him. 'There was nothing you could have done to prevent it.'

Sebastian cut in. 'Señors, there is no point blaming ourselves. We had no idea this was going to happen. This gang had obviously decided to kidnap the señoras. This was just an opportunity. If it had not been here it would have been somewhere else.'

I started to interrupt, but he wasn't finished.

'We don't know who did this thing. But somebody does. I and my men know the people on the streets. The Policía Nacional will do the best job they can, for sure. But they won't have the street people to help them. We will.'

'What do you suggest?' I asked.

'We will need money,' he said, 'lots of it. Señor Gallega is a very rich man, sí?'

'Very rich,' replied Jesús.

'He must be told immediately what has happened and what has to be done.'

I spoke to Jesús. 'We'll need an arsenal.'

'I've only just taken it back,' he complained.

'I know, but we need them back.'

'I'll contact ETA in the morning.'

'I'll get my men on the streets,' Sebastian said. 'We'll try and see if we pick up any leads. These men, they were not Spanish.'

I spoke up, 'The leader, even though I think he was trying to disguise it, spoke with an English accent.'

'I thought that too,' Jesús agreed. 'The Spanish criminal network will not think good of Spanish señoras being kidnapped by foreigners. They will cooperate.'

'Sí. I'm sure of that,' Sebastian said positively. 'That's why I want my men out looking.'

'The ransom,' I said. 'They'll probably contact Señor Gallega. I think someone should go out to him, to be there, see what can be learned. That must be down to you, my friend.' I looked Jesús Alcantara square in the eye.

'Of course. I'll arrange it immediately.'

I was starting to function. 'Sebastian, you know what to do. I'll get a car and go to Puerto Duquesa and poke around. Maybe somebody remembers seeing something. Where's Barbara?'

'Helping with the women,' replied Sebastian. 'Where else?'

'Let's try and give our statements and see if they'll let us leave. Barbara can take care of everything here. The forensic team will probably close the place off anyway. The Jag…'

'Sí, señor?' Sebastian shrugged. 'What?'

'We need wheels. There's my spare. So we need another three. All these cars have spares. There's got to be three that fit. They don't have to match.'

Twenty-four

María Luisa Gallega and Sonia Carabantes were being held on an eighty-foot ocean-going cruiser. They were locked in a cabin, no, more like a stateroom. The windows were blacked out with blinds on the outside.

They hadn't seen the faces of the men who had taken them. They hadn't been harmed and were being well treated.

It was midday, the day after they had been kidnapped.

Yes… *kidnapped*.

It was a terrifying, awful word. In most cases it meant certain death.

They were frightened.

'Chainsaw' Charlie Giles, as he was called, was a career criminal. After a hectic crime spree in England in the eighties, he disappeared to the 'Costa del Crime', as they then called it.

His five partners in crime were not exactly contestants for *Mastermind*.

Lloyd Licorish and Winston Briscoe were black.

Dead black.

They had originally been London bus drivers until they got sucked into a life of crime. They were big, strong and ugly.

Real ugly.

Bruce Delicate was a grey-haired, pot-bellied pig – 'Pot Belly' to his friends. In a former life he sold bacon for a living. Then he realised it was far more profitable to steal it.

By the lorry load.

'Doc' Holliday, real name Dave, was the odd one out of the group. Younger than the others, he was around forty, fit and tanned. He was handsome with well-groomed dark hair.

He had almost completed medical school when he was forced to resign.

'Overfamiliarity with the patients', they called it. One of the charges stated that he was making far too many TUBs. In layman's terms, that meant he was doing far too many 'totally unnecessary breast examinations'.

He still made his living from medicine, however.

Treating the London underworld.

Vic 'the Flick' Smith. A very handy man with a knife. And he liked to use it. A nasty little slimeball. If you owed any money in East London and you heard the name Flick Smith, you paid up. Pronto.

All six were sitting on the stern deck of the cruiser enjoying a cold beer and smoking whatever they fancied. Giles favoured a cigar. It made him feel important.

Doc Holliday didn't smoke. Not healthy.

Pot Belly and Flick smoked cigarettes.

Lloyd Licorish and Winston Briscoe smoked big reefers.

'I can't stand the smell of that shit,' complained Chainsaw.

'Ain't no damn worse dan dat shit you smoking,' Lloyd Licorish retaliated.

'It's also against the law.'

'And you 'spose kidnapping Spanish women ain't, man?' honked Winston Briscoe.

They all burst into peals of laughter at the joke. They all drank. The two blacks high-fived.

After all, it had been a dream kidnapping. They had got clean away. Neither of the women had seen their faces. And wouldn't.

Soon they would make contact for the ransom. 10 million euros – small change to Señor Gallega – for the safe return of his wife.

And safe it would be.

The women would be completely unharmed. Then soon it would be all forgotten. It was a shame about the security man, but after all he was a foreigner. The police would soon forget about him. Then everything would be back to normal.

It was the perfect crime. Nobody could recognise them and they had got clean away.

Kevin Goulding was impressed with the exclusive urbanisation of Sotogrande. And as he sat outside a café on the sparkling new Puerto Sotogrande, he made notes.

He was smoking his third roll-up and nearly finished his second pint of lager. In his little notebook he wrote the name of the boat. He smiled as he wrote it. Someone had a sense of humour: *Crime Does Pay*.

Two blacks.

Four whites.

Two Spanish women on board.

He sat in the warm sun. Gulls swooped for scraps. People wandered along the seafront and the waves lapped gently against the boats. He waved to the waiter for another beer.

And phoned Dooley.

Twenty-five

I got my wheels.

All odd alloys, but who cares. I was on the road.

I was on my way to Puerto Duquesa. My head was full. Sebastian had briefed his comrades and they willingly helped. As always.

Jesús Alcantara had made his dreaded call to Señor Gallega. He took it badly. But he didn't blame Jesús.

Jesús contacted his friends in ETA, who in the circumstances promised to deliver the needed supplies. That left Jesús free to go straight to José Miguel Gallega and be at his side. He would need support when the ransom was demanded.

The police had sealed off the farm as I had expected. It was a crime scene. A murder scene.

Barbara had moved into a de luxe room in a good hotel in San Pedro. She hated Marbella.

The tyre shops were doing a roaring trade. Gradually people got their cars back and the police and forensic teams were able to gather evidence.

Not much, unfortunately.

Liam Dooley arrived back at the Stella Maris in time for breakfast. Johnny McGouldrick was sharing a table of food and a jug of orange juice with Carole and Rita. He called over, 'Liam!'

'God bless all of us,' he greeted. 'It's been a hard night, John.'

'Sure has.'

' 'Tis a shower and a change I'll be needing. We'll need to talk. You missed all the fun.'

McGouldrick laughed, and said in his best Spanish accent, 'I don't fucking think so.'

Dooley laughed tiredly.

'By the pool, auld son. An hour. No booze.'

'To be sure, to be sure.'

Later they sat by the pool and Dooley told him everything.

'Mother o' God!' exclaimed McGouldrick. 'And where in the name o' God is KG?'

'I don't know. I dare not ring him. He might be undercover. I could endanger him. I'll have to wait for him to ring me.'

It was just after midday. Dooley's phone rang. It was Kevin Goulding. Dooley listened intently. 'Good man yerself. Well done, Kevin. Now get back here fast.'

Dooley called over the waiter.

'*Hola, señor!*'

'*Hola.* Two big beers and two Irish whiskeys.'

'Thank fuck for that!' gasped McGouldrick. 'I was dying for a hair of the dog.'

'Well, we won't be doing much today,' said Dooley. 'But make the most of it, 'cause we might just have a busy day tomorrow.

A couple of drinks later, Kevin Goulding arrived.

'Bring the bottle, auld son,' he shouted to the waiter.

The waiter delivered a bottle of Bushmills, unopened, and a glass for Goulding. Dooley dipped in his pocket and stuffed fifty euros in Pedro's hand… if that was his name.

'We'll be needing to be looked after today, auld son. That's for you. Keep up the good work and there's more where that came from.'

Pedro's eyes lit up. '*Sí, señor; muchisimas gracias.*'

'*De nada,*' beamed Dooley, he was picking up the lingo.

Carole and Rita appeared like two beautiful angels, tits wobbling like jellies. McGouldrick jumped to his feet.

'My two little cherubs! Come to your hero. Join us for this hooley of a shindig.'

They squealed with delight. Dooley and Goulding chuckled loudly.

Goulding thought, McGouldrick was never a return ticket.

'My two little Northern Stars,' he beamed. 'I'm obliged to return a favour to yer, for sure.'

'And what would that be?' Rita asked.

McGouldrick had raised his arm, but the cava, ice bucket and two glasses had landed on the table before he could ask.

Pedro knew the score. He filled two flutes. Rita and Carole drank.

'So what's this favour, then?' It was Carole who asked this time.

'Well, last night the two of youse took me to a planet I didn't even know had been discovered.'

'So?'

'So tonight me and me boys are going to do the same for you. Have you ever heard of an Irish Orgy Night? It only normally happens in the green hills of the auld country. But tonight we're going to have the Spanish version. A Spanish-Irish Orgy Night. Can you feel the thrill of it already?'

'You mean all five of us?' exclaimed Rita.

'To be sure. To be sure.'

'Sounds good to me!' howled Carole.

Dooley and Goulding exchanged glances and grinned broadly.

Twenty-six

It took less than twenty-four hours before the ransom demand was received.

10 million euros.

Not an extortionate amount if all the promises were kept. The kidnappers knew the police were involved in the investigation but weren't worried because they knew they had nothing to go on.

Just keep the police out of the ransom payment and they would be happy. They had no wish to harm the women. What would that gain? The women hadn't seen their faces. They couldn't identify them. They were not murderers, just men who needed some money.

Pay the money and the women would be released unharmed.

Simple.

I was wasting my time. I knew that. So I don't know why I was doing it. But I was wandering around Puerto Duquesa asking relatively stupid questions.

I visited the yacht and questioned the crew.

Nothing.

I gave up early and had a beer outside a restaurant. I was thinking when my cell phone rang.

It was Jesús. 'Jack, they have been in contact. 10 million euros and the señoras will be freed unharmed. Señor Gallega has agreed, and asked if we will handle the deal.'

'And they walk away scot free?' I said.

As long as the señoras are safe and well, señor, what difference does it make? Señor Gallega can afford it, he is a very rich man.'

'I'll tell you what difference it makes. They killed Billy Birmingham in cold blood. And there's no guarantee they'll keep their word. They could just kill the women and take the money.'

'So what are you suggesting?' Jesús asked hesitantly.

'I'm suggesting that yes, we handle the ransom,' I started, 'but also that we take precautions.'

'I don't know,' Jesús said mitheringly. 'If anything goes wrong then it's all our fault. Things are bad enough for me as it is, señor. At least if we give them the ransom and it goes wrong after that, we cannot be blamed.'

'Christ, I can't think!' I complained. 'Leave it for now, and I'll meet you at the hotel in San Pedro tonight. We'll talk it over then.'

Twenty-seven

It was almost noon.

The Spanish-Irish Orgy Night had been a resounding success, Dooley thought, as he woke up naked on the floor of Johnny McGouldrick's room.

The two Northern Stars, as they were known, were crashed on the bed, legs akimbo, spark out. The room was like a landfill site. Clothes and bottles and glasses were strewn everywhere. KG and Mr McGoo were sat up on the floor, backs against the wall.

Dooley was completely and utterly fucked. There was a Bushmills bottle with two inches left in it on the table. He took a swig and grimaced. But it did make him feel better. Just.

'God help us all!' he cried, just loud enough to wake everybody.

Rita and Carole grunted out of their slumber. Seeing their bodies naked, they grabbed for something to cover themselves.

'It's a bit fucking late to be worrying about yer modesty,' Dooley choked. 'Get yer arses out of here while we clear up.'

Looking somewhat offended, they slipped on their previous day's bikinis and slammed the door behind them.

Goulding and McGouldrick clambered awkwardly to their feet. They looked strangely stupid, all three of them standing there naked.

'That was one hell of a Spanish-Irish Orgy Night!' howled McGouldrick. 'Give me that bottle yer have in yer hand.'

Dooley passed it. 'Might as well. The day's fucked now.' He shrugged. 'Just promise me one thing.'

'What's that?'

'Take it easy tonight. We gotta see Reec tomorrow.'

They lounged on sunbeds by the pool for the afternoon. They took dinner in the restaurant and then sat comfortably in the hotel bar, sticking just to the beer.

Carole and Rita arrived dressed up, expecting another free

night. They were disappointed. McGouldrick had no more use for them and blew them out.

They looked offended.

'A pair of auld hewers if ever there was one,' he declared self-righteously.

'To be sure. To be sure,' echoed the other two.

All three laughed.

The next morning, they were fit and rested. They filed into the Volvo after breakfast. And drove towards the farm.

It was still a sealed crime scene.

'I'll walk down,' declared Dooley. 'See what's goin' on.'

He was soon back.

'They're staying in San Pedro,' Dooley told them.

It wasn't hard to find the Don Pedro. It was a four star hotel with large pool area and spacious, well cared for gardens.

The three Irishmen were dressed casually in summer slacks and T-shirts. From the reception to the restaurant to the terrace outside, the friendly Spanish señorita eventually pointed out Jack and Barbara.

Dooley made the introductions.

'I believe you're Jack Reec,' he began. I stood up and we shook hands. 'I'm Liam Dooley, this is Kevin Goulding and this scoundrel is Johnny McGouldrick.'

I shook their hands also.

'And who might this beautiful young colleen be?'

'Barbara, my girlfriend,' I answered.

'Yer a very lucky man, Jack, sure you are. A rare gem in a mountain of rock.'

'So what can I do for you?' I asked.

'Well, Jack, we've got a lot to talk about and I don't really know where to start.'

'Be easier if you sat down,' I said.

So they did. McGouldrick next to Barbara. They chatted and laughed. She seemed at ease, and a two-way conversation developed. McGouldrick oozed Irish charm.

Dooley began. 'Can you recall meeting a few friends of ours, some time ago. I believe they came calling on yer.'

'I get a lot of visitors.'

'Irish visitors?'

'Got three now.'

'So you have, so you have.'

'They coulda had two blacks with 'em.'

'I'm sure I'd have remembered.'

'I'm sure I would too.'

'So where's this going?' I asked.

'Well, ye see, we can't find 'em,' Dooley scratched his head. 'Just disappeared.'

'It happens,' I said.

'Anyway, forget about that for now,' he said dismissively. 'This kidnapping thing.'

He'd startled me, as I'm sure he had intended to.

'What do you know about that?' I demanded.

'A lot more than you, I'm sure, auld son.'

Dooley started building a cigarette. I was getting impatient. I felt my voice getting louder.

'Don't fuck about. This is important.'

'Language in front of the lady, please! Be patient.'

'I haven't got time to be patient,' I snapped.

Very deliberately, Dooley said, 'Well, you're going to have to be, auld son.'

He lit his roll-up.

'While we're talking about being patient... these friends of mine, you sure you don't remember them?'

'You don't mean the ones that came to kill me with AK47s in the middle of the night. Shot the two blacks in the back and ended up cut to ribbons all around my garden.'

'Sounds just like 'em!' Dooley laughed. 'Just like 'em.'

'Now I remember them.'

'Sure, I knew you would, Jack. Back shooters one and all. No balls.'

'So what's all this to you?' I asked.

'Well, Jack,' Dooley started, 'somebody's took it real personal and they're willing to pay a lot of money to even the score. Me, I couldn't care less about the gobshites.'

'So what's it all about?'

'The money, Jack,' said Dooley, casually taking a drag. 'But to be honest, Jack, I'm not really a hired killer. I killed a lot of men, but for the cause. Not just for money.'

Kevin Goulding was leaning back in his chair smoking and just listening. Barbara and McGouldrick were chatting away, not seeming to notice what was going on.

Dooley continued. 'Then this other thing cropped up. The kidnapping, I mean. I saw a much bigger cake on the plate. So how much do they want?'

'Who?' I asked.

'The kidnappers.'

'I don't know yet.'

Dooley got to his feet.

'Don't fuck with me, Jack. I'll get my money one way or the other. If not from the ransom, then by blowing you away. Either way I win.'

'What do you know?'

'How much is the ransom? Tell me now or I walk out of here. And you'll never hear of me again. You won't even hear the sound of the bullet that takes off the top of your head.'

'Sit down.'

He did.

'10 million euros. María Luisa Gallega is the wife of José Miguel Gallega, a hugely rich and powerful man. She was with her friend Sonia Carabantes. They were in the care of my friend, Jesús Alcantara. We had organised a huge party on Saturday. Then six men with automatic weapons killed a security guard and kidnapped the women.'

'I know all that, Jack,' Dooley replied. 'I saw it all. Now here's the deal. You can pay the 10 million and maybe never see the women alive again. Or you can pay me 5 million and I'll take you straight to them. I'll even help you get them back.'

'You know where they are?' I gasped incredulously. 'But how?'

'Well, you English seem to have this idea that all Paddys are thick Irish cunts. Wrong, auld son. We were casing the farm and watching the shindig. Great party, by the way. We saw it all. So I says to Kevin here, follow 'em and don't lose 'em. He didn't.'

He let it all sink in.

Then I said, 'Noel Edmunds. That quiz show. What does he say?'

'Deal or no deal?'

'Deal.'

Twenty-eight

Barbara was getting on my nerves.

I was trying to recall and digest everything that Dooley had said. There was a lot to think about.

'He was one of the most interesting men I've ever met,' she enthused. 'And so charming.'

She obviously hadn't got a clue what had been going on. She just seemed to have been hanging on every one of McGouldrick's words.

'He was high in the IRA, you know.'

'Yes, I know.'

'But now that the Troubles are over he's just enjoying the quiet life.'

'Yes, I can see that.'

'I think he's a bit of a darling on the quiet.'

'Fancy him, do you?'

'Jack!' she exclaimed. 'Are you jealous?'

'No, I'm not fucking jealous,' I said in a slightly raised voice, 'but he was sent here to kill me, and all you keep telling me is what a nice bloke he is.'

She looked startled and a little shocked. Thankfully Jesús Alcantara arrived, coming to my rescue.

'*Hola, amigo,*' he said.

'*Hola.*'

'You said it was urgent.'

'Yes,' I replied, and told him everything.

'I'm sorry, Jack,' he said, desperately serious, 'but you cannot do this. You must hand the information to the police.'

I knew he was right.

But it was all so complicated.

Then Sebastian Aparicio arrived. I went all over it again.

He sighed a deep sigh.

'Amigos, have you seen the time? It's gone noon. My mouth is as dry as a kangaroo's pouch. We need beer.'

He called the waiter, and soon there were three large beers and a chilled glass of wine on the table.

After a drink he spoke again. 'Of course Jesús is right. It must be left to the police.'

'The Irishmen won't tell us where the gang are without 5 million euros,' I said. 'So there's the first stumbling block. And we don't have any time to waste.'

'Can we trust them?' asked Sebastian.

'How do I know?' I shrugged.

'We have no choice,' Jesús said. 'How do they want to do it?'

'Wire the money to an account they have, then they tell us everything,' I told him. 'I said we would meet them at three this afternoon at their hotel.'

Sebastian Aparicio took over. 'As soon as we have the information I'll pass it straight on. An operation will be quickly organised.'

Jesús spoke again. 'The weapons I have asked for will be here within the hour. We will take them with us. The Irishmen will not be out of our sight until the two señoras are free.'

Twenty-nine

On board the eighty-foot cruiser *Crime Does Pay*, the celebration was continuing.

Lloyd Licorish and Winston Briscoe were working their way through a bottle of Cockspur Rum.

'Man, dis is sure the life, hey Winston,' enthused Lloyd Licorish.

'De best, man.'

High fives!

Chainsaw Charlie Giles relit his huge cigar for the umpteenth time. Through a haze of stinking blue smoke, he said, 'I've been thinking. Thinking about the women.'

Doc Holliday was about the only one listening.

Bruce 'Pot Belly' Delicate was swallowing his thousandth can. Flick Smith couldn't give a shit.

'And what?' asked Holliday.

'I think we should move them,' he replied thoughtfully. 'You can't be too careful.'

Holliday was the only other brain cell on the boat.

'You think there could be something wrong?'

'Doesn't hurt to be careful, my son. Always cut the odds if you can.'

'Sure. What you got in mind?'

'I think we should transfer them to the smaller boat and take them out to sea. More private.'

'You want me to do it?' Holliday offered. 'These lot are wasted.'

'They're fucking useless when they ain't wasted,' Charlie growled. 'Now, I'll tell you what to do. Go fetch the forty-footer from across the port and moor it next to us. After dark transfer the women and take the two wogs for muscle.'

'Hey, man! Don't you call me no wog, man,' complained Winston Briscoe.

'Dat's right, man!'

Chainsaw Charlie ignored them as if they weren't there. 'These other two pieces of shit can book into a hotel in the town. I'll stay on the boat alone.'

'Sorted.'

Thirty

The bar and lounge in the Hotel Stella Maris was deserted in the afternoon. All of the residents were out in the sun.

The barman was filling his time cleaning and polishing mirrors and glasses. It would get better at around five.

Happy Hour.

The three Irishmen sat around a large square table with four sofas. Only Jack and Jesús had come. Sebastian was still on duty ticketing tourists.

Surprisingly, there were no drinks on the table.

'We were waiting for yer,' Johnny explained. 'What is it you'll be havin'?'

It was beer all round.

Johnny McGouldrick flashed that infectious smile of his. ' 'Tis a fine young wench you have there, Jack. She'd make a welcome guest in anybody's fantasy, to be sure.'

'And fantasising is as close as you're ever going to get to her,' I snapped, instantly regretting that I'd taken the bait.

' 'Twas only a compliment I was payin' ya, Jack.' McGouldrick grinned, spreading his hands.

Kevin Goulding was rolling a cigarette as Dooley raised his hands in the air.

'Children, children! Surely we have more important things to discuss.'

'The money's been transferred,' I retorted.

'I'll check.'

Kevin Goulding was licking down his paper. 'If the man says so,' he drawled.

Liam Dooley got out of the sofa. With his cell phone in his hand he moved out of earshot.

He was soon back.

'It's done,' he confirmed.

'So where are they?' I demanded.

'Easy, auld son,' soothed Dooley. 'You'll be doing yourself a damage. Over to you, Kevin.'

All eyes turned on Kevin Goulding. Coolly, he lit his roll-up and had a smoke.

Slowly he began.

'Well, as our great leader said...' Goulding took another drag and Dooley wore a thin grin... 'our great leader said, "Follow 'em, Kevin, and don't lose 'em." So I didn't.'

Goulding took another drag and a drink of his lager and settled back in the sofa. I tried hard to contain my frustration.

'So I follows 'em. No lights. Long trip, I might tell you. And unfamiliar territory at that. But I never lost 'em. And they didn't see me. I'm sure of that.'

'How do you know?' I demanded.

'Since they wouldn't be after havin' a party the next day on the boat, if they had.'

'What boat?'

'The one with the women.'

'Where?'

He told me.

I told Jesús.

Jesús phoned Sebastian Aparicio. He had just pulled over a speeding motorist. He was just about to write up a citation, but he put the book away.

'Señor, today it is your lucky day.'

Scattering dirt and stones, he raced away.

Thirty-one

Barbara was pissed off. It wasn't her fault that María Luisa Gallega and Sonia Carabantes had been kidnapped. It wasn't her fault that the farm was a crime scene. And it certainly wasn't her fault that the handsome Irishman had taken a fancy to her.

And no way at all was it her fault that Jack had got jealous.

Anyway, she hadn't done anything.

Had she?

No!

So she was going out. Out on the town.

Sod him...

Most of the main road running through Marbella is named Avenida de Ricardo Soriano, after a Spanish Marquis who was first to promote the town's virtues as a resort to his high society family and friends. A nephew, Prince Alfonso von Hohenlohe of Liechtenstein, bought a small beachside farm just west of the town, which was then living off iron mining and fishing. He built a few chalets and began developing luxuriant gardens. In 1953 it opened as the Marbella Club.

All traces of iron mining has gone. There is a new fishing port, but fewer and fewer fish. The old town has been renovated without spoiling it. It is packed with tempting shops and eating and drinking places. A new town has grown around it and runs down to the seashore and promenade.

Most visitors enter Marbella from the east, and on this edge of the resort is the Puerto Cabo Pino, one of Marbella's newest marinas. Next along is Las Dunas, with a long stretch of beach backed by low dunes and a wooded area. A string of urbanisations such as Hacienda Las Chapas, Marbesa and Elvira around here is followed by the Don Carlos and Monteros hotels (both five star and with extensive grounds) and the new Marbella golf course.

It was here that Barbara chose to spend her rebel night out.

The Hotel Don Carlos was one of the area's top de luxe hotels.

Barbara took a stool at the bar and ordered a Harvey ('Take me to heaven!') Wallbanger. The presentation was perfect. The drink a little strong, she thought. It certainly seemed to be the in place. Everybody seemed to be so upper class. The women in million-dollar dresses and dripping with diamonds. The men wore Armani and Versace, all immaculate. Everyone appeared to have the right social connections.

Suddenly Barbara felt out of place.

What was she doing here?

Maybe this wasn't such a good idea after all.

A young man appeared like a genie from a lamp and sat on the stool next to her. He asked, 'What do you make of them all?'

Barbara was drinking from a straw. She stopped and replied, 'I don't really know. I've only just got here.'

'Resident or tourist?'

'Resident.'

'Ah. You fooled me.'

'How so?'

'Well… well you just look like a tourist. So what do you do?'

'I live with my boyfriend on a farm. He's a salvage diver by trade,' she told him. 'He made a few good finds and is now sort of semi-retired.'

'How fascinating,' the young man replied. Barbara guessed he was twenty-five, tall, fit, dark hair, tanned and handsome. 'Please, beg your pardon, the name's David, David Walker.'

Barbara responded, 'Barbara Reec.' They shook hands. Why she said Reec she didn't know.

'Do you mind if I sit by you?' David asked. 'I'm finding this place rather boring, until now. So where's your boyfriend tonight?'

'Working on something very important.'

'To do with his work?'

'I think so. Don't know, really,' Barbara said wistfully. 'To be honest I was feeling a bit pissed off and neglected, and decided to go out on the town for the night.'

'Well, Barbara,' David declared, 'I'm feeling exactly the same. So I'm going to make a proposal. For one night only we are friends. No hanky-panky. We have a bloody good time. We can enjoy a drink and a meal, have fun – on my unlimited expense account, of course. Then I get you a taxi and you go home. Deal?'

'Deal.'

David ordered all the food. The restaurant and service at the Don Carlos were sensational. The food he chose was native Spanish, a mixture of meats and seafood. The champagne was exquisite. Not that Barbara would have known any different. The 1966 Sandeman vintage port was heaven. Nibbling on a superb mixture of cheeses, Barbara was in a suspended state of ecstasy.

'That was the most wonderful meal I have ever had in my life,' she declared, with eyes almost closed.

'It is possibly one of the best meals I've ever had too, Barbara,' he said slowly, reaching across the table to rest his hand on hers. 'But it is undoubtedly the best companion I've ever had. You are simply amazing. I shall remember this night for the rest of my days as the pinnacle of my life. I can never better it.'

Barbara was overwhelmed with emotion, and slightly tipsy. But she felt so happy.

'Thank you, David, I'll never forget it too.'

Elevating the conversation, David said, 'This cheese is too good to waste. I think it needs another glass of port.'

He waved his arm.

The highly trained waiter delivered two more 1966 Sandeman vintage ports.

'To the rest of your life, Barbara. May it be a happy one,' David toasted.

What's left of it, anyway.

Thirty-two

Chainsaw Charlie was bathing in the moonlight with a tumbler of Southern Comfort in his hand on the rear deck of his ocean-going cruiser *Crime Does Pay*.

A whole spit-roast guineafowl was on a plate beside him, from which he was cannibalising bits – leg, wings and chunks of breast.

The two women were safely out at sea with Doc Holliday and the two dumb darkies. The other two useless pieces of shit were in a hotel on the front.

Charlie was enjoying the peace and quiet.

Not for long!

In the blink of an eye, the boat was illuminated like Wembley Stadium on a night game. What Charlie could only assume was the Spanish equivalent of the SAS stormed on board, screaming orders at… Charlie couldn't tell who, making an unearthly noise, like he'd last heard on TV during the siege of the Iranian Embassy… then silence, and at least ten automatic weapons were pointing at him from everywhere.

He plucked a shred of guineafowl breast, ate it and had a sip of Southern Comfort.

'*Buenas tardes, amigos*. Can I help you?'

In perfect English, the officer in charge said, 'I have information that you have two Spanish señoras prisoner on this boat.'

'Well, it's the first I've heard of it, my son. But you're more than welcome to take a look. By the way, I feel slightly uncomfortable with an arsenal of guns aimed at me. It's spoiling my appetite.'

'My apologies, señor.' He waved his hand and the guns lowered.

'*Gracias, señor*,' replied Charlie. Waving his hand he added, 'Be my guest.'

It didn't take long to search the boat. There was no trace of María Luisa Gallega or Sonia Carabantes.

'Can I offer you a drink?' Charlie asked the officer.

The officer dismissed his men. They casually disappeared. The officer removed his cap. 'May I offer you my apologies, señor. An obvious mistake has been made. What you drink will be good for me too.'

Charlie poured him a large Southern Comfort.

'I presume you have a warrant and all the necessary paperwork for this visit?'

Looking a little uncomfortable, the officer replied, 'It was a little bit of a hurry job, señor. Information received.'

'Oh well, no harm done, I suppose. We might as well forget all about it. But try not to let it happen again.'

'*Si, señor.*'

Thirty-three

It was a little bit cramped in Dooley's room at the Hotel Stella Maris.

Six men and three handguns. Dooley, McGouldrick and Kevin Goulding were sat at a table with a bottle of Irish whiskey. Sebastian, and Jesús and I were propped up against the wall, holding the guns.

I was livid.

'So where are they?' I spat the question threateningly. 'Charlie Giles was the only person on the boat.'

'Stay calm,' said Goulding coolly. 'It's not a problem. I know he has them. He's obviously moved them to somewhere safer. All we have to do is find them.'

'And how do you propose to do that?' I scowled at him.

'I'll go and ask him, of course.'

'And he'll just tell you?'

'That's what normally happens,' he replied calmly.

McGouldrick laughed.

'Sure, I never saw anyone yet that could resist Kevin's persuasive manner. Did you ever have boiling oil poured into yer ears? Very persuasive.'

Dooley joined the conversation.

'You three can't afford to get involved now. You've fucked the police up once.'

'No! *You* fucked it up with the police!' I shouted.

'Jack,' he cut in. 'Listen. Youse three are too deeply entangled in this mess. Us, nobody knows nuttin' about us. We can go anywhere, do anything. We're anonymous.'

'He is right, Jack,' Sebastian said. 'We must now keep very low. Our credibility is shaken.'

Jesús Alcantara wanted his say. 'Sebastian is right, señor. We can do nothing now that will go unnoticed.'

'And what about the 5 million euros?' I exclaimed. 'They walk out of here and we never see them again.'

'Jack,' said Dooley seriously, 'I am many things, but not a thief. My word is good through the whole of Ireland. Ask anyone. I say I'm going to kill a man. He's dead. And as for the money, even I know you would be crazy to let me leave here with it.'

Dooley picked up his cell phone and made a call.

'Patsy, auld son, is that yerself I'm talking to? Good man. That 5 million euros. Can you send it back from whence it came? Yes, auld son, I know what I'm doin'. I'm trying to stay alive. Good man.'

Dooley ended the call. 'It shouldn't take long. Now can you put those guns down. I saw one of them go off once. It wasn't a pretty sight.'

'Just once?' I asked.

Thirty-four

Bruce 'Pot Belly' Delicate and Flick Smith had returned to the boat. They were sat on the stern deck with Charlie, drinking bottles of San Miguel.

'How could they have known?' asked Pot Belly Delicate.

'It's a mystery to me,' Charlie said with a worried frown. 'I was fucking lucky that we moved 'em.'

'Yeah,' Flick Smith drawled. 'But it's a major worry. Changes the whole shooting match. We got away with it this time, but someone knows and I just don't get it. Who?'

'I know,' growled Charlie. 'I've been racking my brains. It's doin' me head in. We must have been followed, but how? There wasn't a driveable car left.'

'There had to be somebody else,' said Flick Smith. 'Someone we didn't see. Maybe somebody was on perimeter guard. You never thought of that.'

'What do you mean, I never thought of that? I never heard you fucking mention it! Why is it down to mc?'

'Well, you're supposed to be our great fucking leader.'

'Shut the fuck up,' snarled Pot Belly Delicate. 'We've got some serious shit here, and arguing among ourselves is not going to solve anything. What are we going to do? We need a plan.'

All three went silent for a minute and had another drink from their bottles.

'Right,' Charlie ended the silence. 'We were incredibly lucky last night. No doubt about that. Whoever knew that the women were here couldn't have known that they were transferred to the smaller boat. Or else they wouldn't have bothered storming us.'

'So,' said Flick Smith, 'they can't know where they are now.'

'Even we don't know that yet,' chipped in Pot Belly. 'We know they're out at sea, but as yet not where.'

'That's good for the moment,' said Charlie. 'Whoever it is

only knows about this boat, so I reckon we should get the fuck out of here sharpish and evaporate for a day or two.'

'Yeah,' agreed Flick Smith. 'But what ties us to the boat? Can it be traced to us?'

'Absolutely nothing,' declared Charlie. 'I rented it for a month, paid cash, all false IDs and papers.'

'So the quicker we get out of here the better,' snapped Pot Belly. 'Every minute is crucial.'

'Well, let's not be too quick,' warned Flick Smith. 'Let's make sure we leave the place clean. Don't leave a thing that might tie in to us. I'm starting wiping the place clean of prints, as best I can.'

They all went to work and were so busy they didn't notice the three Irish visitors.

Until Dooley spoke.

'Abandoning ship, are we?'

Dooley filled the door to the spacious stateroom they were busy in. All three men turned, startled.

'Who are you?' demanded Charlie.

'Silent partners, auld son,' Dooley said calmly.

'Partners in what?'

'Crime, of course.'

'What crime?'

'Kidnapping, of course.'

'I don't know what you're talking about.'

'Bit greedy, ten mill... I settled for five.'

It dawned on Charlie that the game was up.

'So what's the deal?' he asked.

'Just tell me where they are. Simple. No probs.'

'And what's in it for me?' Charlie asked nervously.

'You get to stay alive and we just forget all about it, auld son.' Dooley emphasised the 'auld son'.

'I've got a big investment in this,' Charlie snapped angrily.

Dooley put on his most thoughtful frown and appeared to be thinking deeply. 'Have yer never bought yerself an insurance policy or an endowment?'

'Yes.'

'Well what's the last thing the salesman says as you sign on the line?'

'Dunno.'

'He always says that shares can go down as well as up.'

'So.'

'Yours just went down, auld son.'

Flick Smith's knife appeared so fast in his hand that Dooley didn't even see it.

He didn't have to.

The silenced Glock puffed twice from under Dooley's arm as Kevin Goulding put two bullets straight through Flick's heart.

'Dangerous little gobshite,' said Dooley, taking the makings of a cigarette from his pocket.

'Now where were we? Yeah. Share prices.'

Thirty-five

Out at sea, the forty-foot cruiser *Ellabella* bobbed gently on the waves at anchor. Doc Holliday had made no radio contact with *Crime Does Pay*. It was safer that way.

María Luisa Gallega and Sonia Carabantes were growing more fearful for their lives. They were now in mid-ocean. Also, on the smaller boat things were less comfortable.

They started to complain.

Doc Holliday was the only one in contact with them. He always wore his hood.

He kept the two blacks away. They were permanently pissed and a bit of a liability.

Holliday fed them well and reassured them that they would be fine, as he had no doubt that they would be. He reminded them that they had their own private facilities, and as far as kidnapping went, things weren't so bad.

He managed a smile out of them.

Dusk was falling like a transparent silk sheet. The smells of the sea filled his nostrils: salt, seaweed and fresh air.

The deck area was ample for the three of them. Lloyd Licorish and Winston Briscoe were happily laughing and joking in their native Patwa that Holliday found hard to follow. They were drinking tall glasses of pineapple juice laced with Bacardi and Bajan Cockspur rum – a very rough attempt at a pina colada.

To be fair to them, they had caught some nice fresh fish that afternoon and were cooking it on the open grill with a pot of you know what to go with it.

Doc didn't drink much, he liked wine. He decided to open a bottle of red Rioja. He left it to breathe as he screwed off the top of a San Miguel.

'What's this, man?' Winston's huge white teeth flashed. 'You joining the party! Hey, that's great.'

'You know much about West Indian food?' Lloyd Licorish asked.

'To be honest, boys, I don't,' Holliday confessed.

'Well, you sure got some treat comin' to you tonight' boy,' beamed Winston.

'I'll look forward to it.'

High fives all round.

'I could do with freshening up,' Holliday said. 'I feel really minging. Have I got time for a quick dip?'

'Course, man, de dinner got twenty minutes yet. Clean ya self up.'

Doc Holliday stripped naked and carefully dived into the water. It wasn't exactly cold, but it certainly wasn't warm. He swam about, rubbing his body with his hands to clean it. He was cleaning around his foreskin when he felt it getting slightly aroused. He hadn't had sex for a long time and thought about masturbating.

He decided not to.

He climbed back onto the deck by the stern ladder. There was no sign of the blacks. He guessed they were dishing up the dinner.

Before he could dry off he heard raised voices from the far end of the boat. Alarmed, he ran through the galley and the mid section to the bow section where the women were held.

Shit!

The two blacks were in the women's quarters.

'Hey missy, just a little kissy,' he heard.

'You telling me you ain't never had no black man's cock before, missy?'

'Come on, now! We ain't gonna hurt none, missy. It's just a little prick.'

Howls of laughter.

Holliday burst in.

'Get the fuck out of here, you stupid black bastards!'

They scarpered past him quickly, grumbling, apologising, mumbling God knows what.

'I am so sorry about this, señoras. It won't happen again.'

It was then that he remembered that he was naked.

And they weren't looking away… from his lean, fit and tanned body, glistening wet.

'Excuse me, please.'

He turned quickly, making his way to the stern deck, stopping only once to collect a handgun from a cupboard. He burst onto the deck, where he found the blacks looking frightened.

They saw the gun.

'You fools! You've ruined everything. They've seen our faces.'

Holliday brandished the gun. 'Over the rail.'

They stood at the rail facing the sea.

'You stupid black cunts, you've wrecked everything. Well, over you go.'

'You can't leave us out here to drown,' pleaded Lloyd Licorish.

'I wouldn't dream of it.'

Holliday shot him at point blank range, propelling him and his shower of blood, brain and bone with him, over the side into the sea.

Winston Briscoe screamed with terror.

'Stupid black bastard!' Holliday snarled, and despatched him in the same brisk fashion.

Winston crashed into the water, spewing blood. With a bit of luck the sharks might tidy them up.

Holliday turned into the galley and forked a couple of fish onto a plate. He scraped some flesh off the side of the skeleton with his fork and tasted it.

The dead men were right about the food.

Thirty-six

Holliday put on shorts and a T-shirt and went back to the women's cabin.

They looked frightened.

'Don't be alarmed,' he assured them. 'Would you like some fresh air? There's no longer any point in keeping you in your cabin. You've seen my face, among other things, so there is no longer any point in locking you away.'

'Those men?' asked María Luisa Gallega.

'They won't bother you again,' he told them. 'There is fresh hot food in the galley. Come with me. Do you like red wine?'

'*Sí, señor*,' said Sonia Carabantes. 'I love it.'

'Good. Let's try some home cooked West Indian food and Spanish red wine.'

The next thirty minutes were a little tense. All three sat on the deck and finished the food and wine. Doc Holliday had already opened another bottle.

'So,' started María Luisa Gallega, 'the black men. I heard the shots.'

'So you know.'

'*Sí.*'

'So what is there to say?'

'Nothing, I suppose.'

'So forget them.'

Sonia Carabantes sounded alarmed. 'But we have now seen your face and are witness to two murders. That is very bad for us, señor.'

'Could be, I suppose. But I'm sure we can work it out.'

'I would like to think so,' added María Luisa Gallega.

'Listen to me,' said Doc. 'Nobody ever intended for you to get hurt from the beginning. Nothing's changed there. We just want the money. You want to go free. But the blacks have complicated it all by you seeing who I am.'

'I care not about your capture, señor. Only my life. As a Spanish lady of noble blood if I give you my word of honour, on a promise, I never break it.

She turned to Sonia Carabantes and said, 'Señora Carabantes is also of noble and aristocratic blood. Like me, honour means more to her than life itself. When we swear on our honour it will never be broken, believe that. Listen to me. I never saw your face. The other things... Well!'

All three laughed and started on the second bottle.

Thirty-seven

'Have you ever walked in the woods and the dunes on a moonlit night, Barbara?' David asked. 'It is one of the most peaceful and sensational things you can do. And do you know something?'

'What?'

'It's free, it costs nothing. How about that! I can't even put it on my expense account.'

'I'll pay for that then,' joked Barbara. 'It's on me.'

David and Barbara strolled through the grounds of the hotel that led to the beach and the dunes and the woods.

The moonlight bathed the trees and sand. It felt opalescent, bright but not shiny. The waves gently lapped and slopped upon the gentle shore line.

Barbara allowed David to hook his arm through hers. She felt relaxed with her new but distant friend. She was beginning to feel guilty about Jack. That she felt so at ease with this stranger. What was she doing here with a man she hardly knew? She'd been pissed off with Jack, true. But she'd never intended to meet and eat with another man.

But she wasn't doing anything wrong.

Was she?

'No hanky-panky,' David had said.

Well, there'd been none of that.

Yet!

She was confused.

She hardly felt the small syringe, as he injected her.

She didn't really feel any different at first. Then just a little immobile.

David supported her to the safety of the woods and helped her to the sand. She knew everything that was going on. But she was immobile. And worse than that, she couldn't speak.

She couldn't make a sound.

This is the pinnacle of my life, thought David. *Enjoy it.*

He didn't want to hurt her, at first. He looked down into her frightened face and reassuringly stroked her cheeks.

He took off all his clothes and laid them carefully under a tree. Then he gently took off all of hers.

He was throbbing by now.

Barbara was totally paralysed. He parted her legs and kneeled down in the sand, between them.

He hadn't killed anyone for over six months. But the voices in his head were driving him crazy.

One voice told him, 'No, don't do this.' The other voice told him, 'Yes, you must!'

Well, both voices would have to wait…

He would decide later.

For now, it was pleasure.

He slipped his fingers inside her to loosen her up and moisten her. Then, kissing her like a tender lover, he wormed his way inside her. Soon he had found his rhythm. And he could see she was loving it.

'More, more!' she was silently screaming. He could see it on her face.

He buried himself deeper until he knew she'd had her ultimate climax.

'Kill her, kill her!' screamed the voice in his head. 'You haven't killed for six months.'

He retrieved a small case from the pocket of his jacket. He took from it a medical scalpel.

He knelt down again between her parted legs on the sand. The scalpel glistened in the moonlight. He sliced beneath each breast and pushed them back. Blood gushed down her torso.

He gained another erection and immediately used it.

What a way to die, he thought.

He drew the scalpel across the abdomen, caesarean-style. Then from the inside out he cut up to the incision.

The screaming voices wanted more blood, but there was no more.

David Walker was a psychopathic killer. He could do nothing about it. It was like being homosexual. You didn't fucking want to be, but you were.

He collapsed on the body for a while. Then, as the voices faded gently in his head, he started to revive.

It was messy. He was covered in blood. He pulled himself together and set about clearing up. He dragged Barbara by the arms across the sand into the sea. He towed her out as far as he could until he felt a strong current pulling away from the beach.

He let her go and washed himself clean, then swam back to the beach. He dried himself with Barbara's clothes then dressed. He gathered Barbara's clothes into a ball and wandered back to the hotel. Along the way he found a waste bin and pushed them to the bottom. What was in the bottom he dragged over the clothes to cover them.

David was his immaculate self as he re-entered the bar of Hotel Stella Maris.

'Small beer, large Scotch.'

The voices in his head had been pacified.

For now!

Thirty-eight

The forty-foot cruiser, *Ellabella*, bobbed gently at anchor in the middle of the Mediterranean Sea. It was early morning and the mist was beginning to burn away, leaving warm, clear blue skies.

Doc Holliday was drinking coffee and breakfasting on eggs and toast. He was quite a handsome man and looked fit in his brightly coloured Bermuda shorts. He was thinking about the two women and the very pleasant evening he had spent with them. They were definitely very beautiful, articulate and aristocratic. It was no hardship to spend some time with them.

But the whole thing now was a complete fuck-up.

At least the blacks were gone. No loss; they were only muscle. He still hadn't heard from Charlie, which made him think that something else could be going wrong.

He had some more coffee.

María Luisa Gallega had read or heard somewhere that in a hostage situation it was best to try and form some kind of bond with your captors. She discussed it with Sonia Carabantes, who wholeheartedly agreed.

They wandered to the stern of the boat where Holliday was sitting.

'*Buenos dias!*' They both greeted him together.

'Good morning, señoras.'

They were still dressed in the clothes they had been captured in. Sonia Carabantes said, 'As you can see, señor, we are a little short of clothing. Are there any swimsuits, shorts or T-shirts anywhere?'

'Yes, sure. There's a chest in the main cabin area,' he told them. There's loads of spare stuff in it. A lot of girls come to play on the boat. Just help yourself. As for food and drink, just do whatever you want. Treat the place as your own.'

'You are very kind, señor,' said María Luisa Gallega. 'We have not yet been properly introduced. I am María and this is Sonia. And you, señor, are?'

'My friends call me Doc. So Doc should do.'

'I am not too sure about the level of our friendship.' Sonia laughed. 'But Doc it is.'

María said to Sonia, 'Shall we see what clothes we can find? I feel a little overdressed for a cruise at sea. We will be back shortly… Doc.'

Holliday sat back in his chair and luxuriated in the sun and the beautiful calm blue sea. He raised himself out of his seat and leaned on the rail, gazing down into the crystal clear depths. He was transfixed in his thoughts when María spoke and startled him. He jumped up and swung around quickly.

'We found something.'

She and Sonia were wearing bikinis. One pink, one yellow. 'What do you think?'

'A perfect fit, I'd say,' Doc said admiringly. 'In fact they could have been made for you.'

He made no attempt to disguise the fact that he was impressed with what he saw. Both women had ample breasts and narrow waists over tight, flat stomachs. They had long slender legs and were tanned the colour of fine antique furniture.

'May I compliment you both on your great beauty,' he told them. 'I don't think I could have kidnapped two more beautiful women if I had targeted the Miss World pageant.'

'Which allows me to ask,' said Sonia, winking, 'what do you intend to do with us?'

'Well, in light of the new situation,' Holliday grinned, 'I could tell you what I'd like to do with you.'

'I think perhaps you should keep that to yourself,' countered María.

'What a pity,' Doc shammed disappointment. 'I was looking forward to that.'

Thirty-nine

'Chainsaw' Charlie Giles stared in shock at the suddenly dead body of Flick Smith.

Bruce 'Pot Belly' Delicate was frozen with fear.

It was all so swift and calm, and matter of fact. Goulding was lighting a cigarette, and the third man behind him was laughing excitedly as if they had just won a coconut at the fair.

'Nice one, KG,' he said. 'Slippery little cunt, that one. I hardly saw where the knife came from.'

'Died for nuttin', really,' Goulding drawled coolly. 'He never had a chance.'

'Do you think we should say a prayer for his soul?' asked Dooley. 'And for these other two.'

Kevin Goulding exhaled a rod of blue smoke. 'Not much point, auld son. We know the only place he's goin'.'

'Just the same,' said Johnny McGouldrick, grinning and pushing his way through the door from behind, 'I think maybe, the sign of the cross.'

'Yer an eejit, McGoo,' said Dooley, 'but as you say…'

All three made the sign of the cross.

All very unsettling for Delicate and Charlie.

'Now, where's the women?' demanded McGoo.

'Haven't got a clue,' said Charlie, trying to sound desperate.

Dooley sounded bored and tired. 'Ye know, I can't be arsed with all this. Shoot the other cunt.'

Kevin Goulding raised his gun to Bruce 'Pot Belly' Delicate.

Putting on his best despairing voice, Dooley said, 'Not that piece of shit. *Him.*' He pointed to Charlie. 'He's the *brains.*'

'May Jesus help 'em if he's the brains!' howled McGouldrick.

And suddenly all three of the Irishmen were giving off peals of laughter. Goulding slowly moved the barrel of his gun to Charlie.

They were still laughing when Charlie screamed with terror, '*Stop! No!* I'll tell you.'

Forty

Where was Barbara?

I sat in my hotel room in San Pedro and wondered.

I knew she was pissed off, but she'd never stayed out all night. And she wasn't answering her phone.

I was worried.

I phoned Sebastian Aparicio.

'Amigo, I will do all that I can. Did she give any indication that she was going anywhere?'

'No. We had a few cross words about the Irishman, and I know she was pissed off.'

'Did she take the car?'

'No.'

'So she had to take a taxi.'

'I suppose.'

'So we'll start there.'

'*Gracias.*'

'Keep ringing her cell.'

'I will.'

There was a knock on my room door. I opened it, and found Jesús Alcantara.

'Barbara.' He frowned. 'I am worried. It is not like her.'

'I know,' I said. 'We had a few words, but nothing too serious. She wouldn't stay out all night and not phone me. And she's not answering her phone either. I'm worried.'

'What did Sebastian say?' asked Jesús.

'He's checking all the local taxi firms,' I told him.

As I spoke my cell phone rang. 'She took a taxi to Hotel Don Carlos.' It was Sebastian. 'I'm going there immediately. I'll talk to you later.'

There was full cooperation with the police at the Don Carlos.

Yes, the bar and restaurant staff remembered the young woman – and the handsome young man she dined with…

I was gutted.

They appeared to be having a wonderful romantic evening. Best food, best champagne and what the waiter remembered most, 1966 Sandeman vintage port. The very best.

The bill was paid with cash.

The last sighting of them was walking hand in hand through the hotel grounds to the dunes and the woods, by the beach.

I was now super gutted.

I couldn't believe what I was hearing!

It sounded as if I was being betrayed.

But Barbara wasn't like that!

Was she?

I just didn't know any more.

Sebastian was on his cell phone as he walked the alleged route of the lovers.

Lovers!

The thought of it creased me. I couldn't believe it.

Sebastian passed through the magnificent grounds of Hotel Don Carlos to the dunes and the woods. It was day now, and still there were practically no people around.

A lover's paradise at night, he thought.

He silently reprimanded himself for thinking it.

But what else could it be?

He roamed around looking for anything.

Anything.

He didn't know what.

'Jack, I can see nothing.' He spoke into the phone. 'I'm coming back. Just keep calling her.'

Still looking for anything strange, he meandered back through the dunes to the hotel.

Not far from the perimeter of the hotel grounds he heard the sound of a familiar mobile phone.

It was the Police: 'Every Breath You Take'.

Barbara's…

But where was it coming from?

He strained his ears.

He looked all around.

It seemed to be coming from a trash bin on the sand.

He dug into the rubbish deeply and pulled out a woman's dress and small handbag. In the bag was a cell phone.

He answered it.

'Hello?' he asked.

'Hello,' it answered.

'Is that you, Jack?'

Forty-one

The ship-to-shore radio was out of range.

Doc Holliday switched off his mobile phone.

He needed to save the battery as he didn't have a charger with him.

And he didn't really want to be disturbed!

He was relaxed and having fun.

Enjoying himself, really.

He was sunbathing with María and Sonia on the stern deck, drinking Spanish cava.

It was Sonia who spoke.

'Doc.' She said it as if she didn't feel comfortable with it. 'Would it trouble you if we were to sunbathe topless?'

'Why would it?' he replied.

'I just thought it polite to ask,' she said. 'We normally sunbathe naked, but I'm sure that would be far too embarrassing for you.'

'But why would you think that?' he asked. 'Didn't you know that I am a fully trained doctor? To me the human body is just an amazingly complex machine. Nothing more,' he lied.

'We didn't realise,' María said, entering the conversation. 'So there is absolutely no reason for us to be embarrassed.'

'Of course not. And now that we've cleared that up, I like the all-over myself.' He slipped off his shorts as María and Sonia discarded their bikinis.

'God, that feels great,' Holliday remarked, feeling himself growing slightly in stature.

The afternoon sun was not too warm. It was still early in the year. But it was still warm enough to make you sticky. Holliday wasn't ever really a drinking man.

But he was getting the taste for it. They had just cracked the second bottle of cava and he'd had a San Miguel to quench his thirst.

'I don't know about you,' he said, 'but I could do with a dip.'

And a swim, he joked to himself.

'Great idea,' María enthused. 'I'm hungry too. Do we have a barbecue?'

'Got loads of those disposable ones,' said Doc.

'What about if we have a swim and I do some real Spanish cooking?' piped in Sonia.

'Good with me.'

They swam a while, dried off, and Sonia started to cook.

With a bottle of red wine.

'So what is going to happen to us?' María asked out of the blue.

'I really don't know,' Holliday confessed. 'I'm in over my head. I'll never hurt you, but to be honest I think I'm in the shit. If I could put the clock back I'd never have got involved.'

'So why don't we just phone my husband and he will rescue us?'

'If only it was that simple!' he groaned. 'But we're talking kidnap here.'

'But what if you were my rescuer. A hero. The one who saved us. I'm sure my husband would be grateful. And I'm sure there would be a generous reward.'

Holliday was thinking. *Hard.*

It could work.

After all, he'd killed the blacks.

The smells of Sonia's marvellous cooking swept over the deck of the *Ellabella*.

The sight of these two amazingly beautiful Spanish women was getting a little too much for Holliday.

As María could see…

There was a lot less chance of being raped if he'd been seen to, she thought.

'I think you need a hand with that,' she told him.

'I think you might be right.'

'Come with me!

Forty-two

'Can youse three get yer arses over to this boat before I completely lose me temper!' Dooley barked down his cell phone to Jack. 'I'm blowing these two gobshites away and going home.'

'Stay cool, I'm coming,' I replied, trying to keep him calm.

'Well, you'd better not be fuckin' long.'

'It's not my fucking fault if I can't get through to them,' cried Charlie, almost pleadingly.

'And it ain't mine either.'

Jack, Jesús and Sebastian arrived.

'So what's the problem?' I asked.

'This fuckin' eejit tells me the women are on another boat with three of his men, but he can't get in touch with them!' Dooley shouted.

Jesús Alcantara stepped forward into Charlie's face.

'Is this true, señor?'

'He knows it's true,' Charlie said pleadingly.

'María Luisa Gallega and Sonia Carabantes were placed in my hands for safety, by my best friend José Miguel Gallega,' Jesús said with menace. 'I was entrusted to look after them and you have stolen my honour. Believe me, my friend, if you think you have been treated harshly by my Irish friends, then you can have no idea of the consequences you have drawn upon yourself.'

Johnny McGouldrick started to laugh. He said to Charlie, 'Sure, boyo, I thought 'twas a bad time you were havin' with us. It's protectin' you we are.'

The backhand from Jesús that smashed against Charlie's face split his lip and broke his nose at the same time.

The blood splatter flew and landed on Kevin Goulding.

'That was my best bloody shirt!' he roared and crashed the barrel of his gun into Charlie's cheek, ripping it open. 'Now you've got blood all over me gun, you eejit!'

He whacked him over the head again.

'Chainsaw' Charlie Giles broke down in tears.

A sorrowful wreck of a man, allegedly the hardest man on the Costa del Crime.

'I don't know what else to do,' he sobbed.

I didn't either.

Jesús Alcantara's friends had been kidnapped. And Barbara was missing, her clothes and belongings found in a trash bin on the beach.

What was going on?

What were we to do?

Sebastian Aparicio spoke for the first time.

'This violence is getting us nowhere. We have many big problems here. There is a body, for starters. Then these two. What are we to do with them? They can't help us, they say. They are a big problem. Blow them away.'

It was then that Bruce 'Pot Belly' Delicate spoke for the first time. 'The only thing I know is that they transferred the women to a forty-foot cruiser called *Ellabella*. It has to be out there somewhere. So all you have to do is find it. It can't stay out there for ever, can it?'

I knew what he said made perfect sense. And I knew what had to be done.

We had to find Barbara, and we had to find Sonia and María.

The three of us and the three Irishmen took a couple of steps back and huddled into a group.

Kevin Goulding built a cigarette.

Jesús, Sebastian and myself stepped out of the cabin. Goulding lit up.

'Sorry, auld son,' he drawled, 'but at least I'll give it ye in the heart.'

He had a smoke.

The silenced gun puffed twice and 'Pot Belly' Delicate crashed back over a chair, dead.

Two more puffs and so did 'Chainsaw' Charlie Giles.

Forty-three

Sebastian Aparicio arranged for the disposal of the bodies. His cousin worked at the crematorium and sometimes 'did' a foreigner.

This time, three foreigners.

It was a strange alliance.

The three Irishmen had been sent to kill me, but now we were working together.

I thought it strange.

But they wanted 5 million euros. And I and my friends wanted María and Sonia back safely.

All of our lives were intricately entwined, in the same cause.

And also there was Barbara. Where was she?

I was sick with worry.

And truthfully, although I couldn't say it, I cared more about her than the Spanish señoras.

Sebastian was trying to find any information he could on the cruiser *Ellabella*.

The police had finally finished at the farm and I moved back in.

It felt lonely. Empty. I thought of Barbara with a strange, handsome young man. I thought of her eating fine foods, drinking the best champagne, and walking to the beach with someone she didn't know.

Where was she?

Was she with him?

Had she left me for some young man? What had I done so wrong? Or was it just me? I didn't know. It was driving me crazy.

As much as I loved Jesús Alcantara, he seemed preoccupied with his señoras. It was as if Barbara would just turn up.

Sebastian was doing his best to help us both. Without favour.

The Irishmen had gone back to their hotel and were letting off a little steam.

Understandably.

They had, after all, just killed three men.

Not that is seemed to bother them.

But alone on the farm I was miserable.

I was drinking heavily when my cell phone rang.

It was Sebastian.

The coastguard had found the body of a young woman floating in the sea.

Forty-four

Until Barbara, David Walker hadn't killed for six months. But now the voices in his head were urging him on.

It was like sex. You didn't have it for some time, but when you tasted it again you wanted more.

He was already a serial killer. Barbara was his sixth. He never killed in the same place twice, so nobody had ever put it all together.

He'd liked Barbara. He only killed people he liked. And he liked beautiful young girls. He'd killed in England, Brittany, the South of France, Portugal and now Spain.

And now he would kill again in Spain. In Antequera, forty-five kilometres from Malaga.

Antequera had a strategic importance which was recognised by successive conquerors. The Romans left their mark, and so did the Moors. Prince Fernando captured it in 1410 and it became a forward base for the assault on Granada.

But it was La Piedra de los Enamorados (Lovers' Rock) from which two lovers, a Muslim and a Christian, are said to have jumped, in order to be together in death rather than apart in life, which caught David's imagination.

What a romantic place for a wonderful kill!

Sitting outside a pavement café, with a bottle of local white wine in an ice bucket, he watched as the world passed by. Dressed casually smart in light chinos and a crisp short-sleeved shirt, he looked every inch the respectable well-heeled tourist. Shaded from the sun by the table's umbrella, he fought with the dilemmas in his head.

He was two people. He knew that. And he hated it. Why couldn't he just be like everyone else? Just one person. Why couldn't he just dump the second person? And be himself...

But which one was himself?

That was the fucking problem.

Maybe he really was a monster. A killer.

A small coach slowed to a stop across the street. After a few minutes it began to empty. Sleepy-looking tourists emerged in a variety of awful shorts, horrendous tops and old-fashioned dresses. They had all the expected accessories – tatty bags and cheap sunglasses – and they began to disperse and drift off for their browse around the town.

'You have two hours only. Then you must be back at the coach,' instructed the smartly uniformed guide.

She was medium height, slim, brown and beautiful with silky black hair cut in a neat bob.

David Walker liked her.

The guide looked at her watch, checked for traffic and crossed the deserted street to the café.

'*Hola!*' she said, greeting the only person in the place.

David Walker.

'*Hola,*' he replied. 'Beautiful day, as ever. Nice and quiet this time of the year. Don't like it when it gets too busy.'

She was Spanish, but in perfect English she said, 'I certainly don't. It makes my job a lot more difficult.'

David Walker stood. 'Would you like to sit? Or perhaps you would prefer to be alone?'

'I will sit, if you don't mind,' she smiled. 'It will be two hours before the coach leaves.'

She sat down; so did David Walker. He said, 'Would you like a drink?'

'Cappuccino would be wonderful. *Gracias.*'

'I don't normally go around picking people up in the street.' He smiled as he spoke, noticing her huge deep brown eyes.

'I do,' she replied. 'All the time. At least forty people a day.'

They both laughed at that.

'My name is Esther Fernandez.'

'David Walker.'

He really did like Esther Fernandez.

Forty-five

I don't know what it was, but I was convinced that the body recovered from the sea was Barbara. As yet, there was no evidence or reason. It could be anyone. But she was missing, and a body had been found. And she had gone missing by the sea.

I opened another San Miguel and drank from the bottle. I was sitting by the pool in the moonlight. The loneliness and desperation, followed by despair, was beginning to engulf me like a thick sea fog.

I heard the sound of a car coming down the track and turned to see the SLK 200 of Jesús Alcantara crunch onto the gravel.

The two of them got out.

Jesús and Sebastian. I didn't do much to greet them. They looked solemn and glum as they sat at chairs on either side of me.

They didn't have to tell me.

'What happened?' I asked.

'She was murdered, Jack,' Sebastian said, looking away from me.

'How?'

'There will have to be a full post-mortem, but she was cut up pretty bad.'

'How bad?'

'Mutilated.'

'Before or after she died?'

'Can't say until after the post-mortem.'

'Jack...' Jesús Alcantara spoke for the first time. 'Trust me. We will get him. I know we will. I will never rest until he is cut to ribbons for the dog that he is.'

'Who?' I asked.

'Whoever did it, of course.'

'You have problems of your own,' I reminded him. 'You have two kidnapped women to find. You can't do everything.'

'Barbara was my friend.' A tear welled in his eye. 'I loved her like a daughter.'

'I know,' I said, 'but Barbara is dead. The two señoras are alive. It is more important that you find them before they are dead too.'

'I need a drink.' It was Sebastian who interrupted.

He fetched a bottle of Blue Label Smirnoff vodka from the bar with three tumblers and a bucket of ice. He banged it on the table and poured.

After a while, and a lot of melancholy reminiscing, we heard the engine of another car. The Volvo estate crunched through the stones and stopped.

It was the three Irishmen.

'God bless all here!' Dooley called. 'Is it a party you be havin'? And without us! How could yez?'

'Grab your choice of bottle from the bar,' I called. 'There's Bushmills somewhere, if you look.'

They found it and pulled up chairs around the others.

'And where's my beautiful Barbara?' boomed Johnny McGouldrick with his huge white-toothed grin. 'It'll be no party without her.'

I told him.

Tears welled in his eyes. I could feel the emotion building up in him. It was like a boiling steam kettle. He flung his glass across the garden. He smashed his fist against the table, spilling two glasses and rocking the rest. And then he screamed it.

'On me sacred mother's grave, I swear to you, Jack Reec, that we'll find the louse-bound fucking bastard who did this, and we'll kill the cunt, slowly cutting him to pieces. On me sainted mother's life, I swear it.'

Everyone looked shocked.

And I believed him.

Forty-six

On board the *Ellabella* Doc Holliday was beginning to think it strange that he'd had no communication from Charlie.

Not that he was particularly bothered. Life on board was pretty good. He was thinking hard over what María had said. About being a hero, getting a reward and being a rescuer instead of a kidnapper. In theory it sounded great. But practically, how could you make it foolproof?

He knew what they were up to, and he was going along – who wouldn't? The afternoon interlude had been a pleasantly erotic experience, even if she had only done it to survive. She had certainly enhanced her chances, that was for sure.

As the afternoon merged into evening, Holliday and the women washed in the sea and put on some clothes for the evening. He was cooking a chilli con carne in the galley and sipping red wine.

I'm getting too much of a taste for the booze, he thought.

After dinner it felt a little cold. A bit of a breeze had sprung up and there was a chill to it. María suggested that they retire to the comfort and warmth of the main cabin. All agreed.

Holliday seemed a bit fidgety. 'So how do you think it will work if I let you phone your husband?'

'I will tell him you never really wanted to get involved with it. That you protected me and even killed the two black men who were pestering us,' she said simply.

'Sounds great,' said Holliday, 'and not so far from the truth. So the reward. How does that work, and how much?'

Thoughtfully, María said, 'I do not know. I would have to speak with my husband. What would you have in mind?'

'This is all getting too crazy,' Holliday moaned. 'I need to speak to Charlie.'

'What can he do?' snapped Sonia Carabantes. 'Forget the others! They are no longer a part of this. You have rescued us.

You are a hero. You can have nothing to do with them. Just think of yourself. You take the reward, as we shall call it, and disappear.'

'Sonia is right, Doc,' María said earnestly. 'You cannot be a hero and still be part of them. Cut them loose. Go free. With them you are condemned.'

'OK,' Holliday said. 'Back to the reward. The ransom was 10 million euros. So a reward is twenty per cent. I make that 2 million. *Cash.*'

'I'll talk to José Miguel.'

'Do that.'

He handed her his cell phone. 'I want to hear your every word.'

'Of course, señor.'

'Keep it short. Just the basics.'

He listened as she spoke and ended the call.

'My husband is happy with the reward, and offers you his wholehearted thanks for saving our lives. He will be forever in your debt. And he awaits your arrangements.'

She passed him back the cell phone.

'I don't know yet.'

Forty-seven

David Walker had truly enjoyed his two hours talking to the beautiful Esther Fernandez. As he dressed in his hotel room, preparing for their dinner date, he reflected upon the time they had spent together and the information they had both learned about each other.

Esther Fernandez was a tour guide, obviously, and lived in Antequera. She was unmarried and did not have a boyfriend. She had her own nice, compact two-bedroom apartment and she was only too happy to accept the offer of dinner with the charming David Walker.

He didn't know the town so she chose the restaurant. She went with seafood. A good choice. They met in the bar and had cocktails as they ordered.

Bloody Marys.

'So what brings you to Antequera?' asked Esther.

'I am looking for locations for a film that I'm going to direct,' he lied.

'So that's what you do then.' Esther sounded impressed.

'Yes,' he lied again, 'but it's not as glamorous as it sounds. It's just damn hard work.'

'I am sure you are just being modest. It must be a wonderfully interesting career.'

'Sometimes, I suppose.'

The waiter interrupted.

'Your table is ready. Will you follow me please?'

They left their almost finished Bloody Marys and followed the waiter to a nice private table in the corner of the almost empty restaurant.

It was spotlessly set with a crisp white tablecloth. A bottle of champagne was open in a silver-plated bucket. The waiter seated them both.

'Shall I pour, señor?' the head waiter asked.

'*Gracias.*'

'Would you like to taste it, señor?'

'I'm sure it will be perfect.'

'It always is.'

He filled both flutes and left them. David and Esther raised their glasses and toasted each other. David said, 'To ships that pass in the night.'

'I do hope not.'

'That we can only see.'

They drank.

The waiter returned pushing a trolley with two gas burners. Expertly, he flambéed the giant king prawns in garlic sauce.

The seafood platter was a work of art. The whole sea bass at the centre was the cornerstone of a masterpiece of sculptured fishes and prawns. Two huge crab claws were embedded in the salad.

It was a sacrilege to disturb it.

The waiter stood over the dish, beaming with pride.

'Shall I serve it, señor?'

'Please do,' David Walker told him. 'It is truly *magnífico.*'

He glowed.

To finish the meal, David ordered cheese and biscuits and 1966 Sandeman vintage port.

Esther Fernandez said that it was the best port she had ever tasted.

'My apartment is only a short walk from here,' she told him. 'Would you like to end this beautiful evening with a coffee on my balcony?'

'That sounds a lovely idea. I'd love to.'

As they walked through the door of Esther's apartment she felt a little prick from the syringe.

She hardly noticed it.

But within seconds she was immobilised. David took her weight and carried her to the bedroom. He laid her gently on the bed.

She was beautiful.

He gently undressed her. He caressed her fabulous breasts and licked her nipples. When she was totally nude, he rolled her onto her front and gazed at the magnificent shape of her body.

He ran his hands all over it. Down her back, over her buttocks and down the back of her legs. Then back up the inside of her legs until he couldn't go any further.

At that point he undressed himself and folded his clothes carefully on a chair away from the bed so as not to get blood on them.

The voices in his head were driving him on now.

Whose voice was it now, anyway? Was it his fucking voice or the Devil's?

Who was he?

David Walker?

Lucifer?

He just didn't fucking know!

He raised the lower half of her body up onto her knees.

He entered her gently to give her the greatest pleasure. He could tell she was loving it. She just couldn't say so. He was crying in ecstasy with her now.

What a wonderful time they were both having... *together*.

And then it was over.

And then the voices screamed for the kill.

Thumbs down!

This was the best bit.

Or was it the worst bit?

He didn't know.

Only that he had to do it.

Rolling Esther over on her back again, he used the scalpel swiftly, slashing beneath her breasts. Then across the midriff. Then from between her legs to her belly button.

Blood was shed.

The voices were satisfied.

For now, anyway.

Forty-eight

The post-mortem results on Barbara were ready.

But was I ready?

Sebastian had a full copy of the whole report.

We all sat around the pool in the semi-darkness of evening. It was a wonderfully peaceful night. A gentle earlier shower had dampened the garden and enhanced the smells of fresh earth, leaves and citrus fruit. The taste of the air was like the description of a fine wine that you read on a bottle. It soaked up your nose and landed down on your tongue.

Three Irish, two Spanish, and one man from Jersey in the Channel Islands: me. We all had our drink of choice as we waited on Sebastian's words.

'Amigos,' he began. 'As they say in the bullring, let's cut to the kill. I don't want to drag this through the blood in the sand.'

'Well – don't, then,' urged Johnny McGouldrick. 'Get on with it.'

'Sí. Barbara was drugged with a hypodermic syringe. She was raped, then her breasts were almost severed from her body. Her abdomen was cut open and she was cut from the vagina to the naval. She bled to death.'

'Jesus! I said get on with it! I didn't say to just clinically pour out the details, like she was a piece of meat on a butcher's block,' moaned McGouldrick.

'I'm sorry,' Sebastian apologised. 'It just seemed the easiest way. We are all familiar with death. It happens.'

I said, 'Thanks. It is best to know exactly what happened. There is no easy way.'

Jesús Alcantara was next to speak. 'Amigos, we all know what has been decided. I have to find the two señoras who were in my charge. And I lost. Jack *must* find the killer of Barbara. We will be going our separate ways on our quests. It could be a long road.'

I spoke again. 'As we all decided yesterday, there will be two groups. Myself and Mr McGoo here will begin to hunt down Barbara's killer. Sebastian is to remain between both groups, gathering whatever information he can. Jesús and Liam and Kevin will try to track down the kidnappers. And that's it, really.'

'Well said,' Dooley piped up.

'And I'll drink to it,' said McGouldrick.

'Sure you'll drink to anything!' howled Goulding.

'And why not?' cried Dooley. 'Let's have a hooley tonight. Then work.'

I smiled through my grief at these men who had been sent to kill me and now *seemed* to be my friends.

We drank.

Not partied.

We were melancholy, but we had all seen death so many times before that it was no stranger.

You couldn't put it back. Life.

Only avenge it.

And that was what we intended to do.

Then Sebastian's cell phone rang. He answered it and listened intently.

'There's been another girl killed. A Spanish girl – in exactly the same way. To the letter. It has to be the same man. Jack, we have a serial killer.'

Forty-nine

The murder of Esther Fernandez was the hottest news in Spain. It was immediately linked to Barbara's death, and soon after that, to others. With the whole publicity machine grinding, police forces in other countries, Britain, France and Portugal, compared cases that hitherto had not been linked to each other.

The body count stood at eight.

A seriously deranged serial killer was out there.

Spain was gripped with fear.

Comparisons were being made with the Yorkshire Ripper, even though there was never any suggestion that any of the women had been prostitutes.

It was going 'Whole of Europe'. Huge television coverage. News crews began to descend on the farm.

I was pissed off.

The grief was bad enough.

But this!

I gave them what they wanted. Anything to make them go away.

I made an appeal for information. Made a statement and gave them a photo and some background on Barbara. When they thought they had enough, they left.

And then I was star of the television news. A hot line was set up for any callers with any information about the killings.

There were hundreds of calls.

But no information.

Jesús Alcantara had set out to fulfil his own task, with the help of Dooley and Goulding. I was sat by the pool with my new ally, Johnny McGouldrick.

He was an oasis of hope in a desert of pessimism.

'We'll get the scut for sure, Jack, have no fear of that. He's already makin' mistakes. Until he killed the Spanish girl nobody had ever heard of him. Now the whole of Europe is trying to bite his arse.'

'You're sure right about that,' I said, throwing back another Smirnoff.

'It's a plan we need, Jack,' McGouldrick said, downing a Bushmills. 'And first thing in the morning it's away to Antequera, before the trail goes cold. Yer man won't be stickin' around for long. That Jag of yours should get us there well enough.'

'I bet he's long gone by now,' I said.

'Don't be so sure, Jack. He's an arrogant cocky bastard. Got a lot of front. Probably completely fucked up in the head. Two people, each going in the opposite direction. He doesn't know who he is, any more than we do. But we'll find out. He never will.'

I was amazed. 'But how do you know all that?'

'I met a lot like him in my time, Jack. Cocky little gobshites. Too smart ever to get caught. But they always are. Trust me, Jack, we'll find him, and when I'm finished rearranging him he'll wish he'd been the victim of an abortion.'

He was scaring me!

It was then my phone rang. It was the local radio station that was covering the story. I listened to the presenter. A caller was on the line with really hot information, but would only speak directly to me.

'Would I be put through?'

I had no choice.

'Hello, Jack. It's me. Barbara's last date. She had a wonderful evening. She said the 1966 Sandeman vintage port was the best she had ever tasted. It was all your fault. You pissed her off over McGouldrick.'

The phone went dead.

Fifty

Doc Holliday had figured it out.

A deserted stretch of coast for a handover.

The women, then the 'reward'.

María Luisa Gallega has spoken to her husband again. Everything was cleared. His representatives would meet him at his chosen location, hand over the money, and take the two women.

And he was free.

Well, it didn't always work like that.

So he had plan B.

It wasn't going to be easy on his own. He would be well outnumbered, that was for sure. He had to help the odds.

He needed to get hold of the cash and check it. He had to keep the women until everything was done.

Not so easy.

They sat under an umbrella, shaded from the hot midday sun. They were drinking cold beers and snacking on sandwiches.

'I might as well be straight,' Holliday confessed. 'I'm nervous about a double-cross.'

'I can assure you, Doc,' began María, 'my husband would do nothing that would endanger my life. He just wants me back. Safely.'

'Unfortunately, the police may be involved and see things differently,' countered Holliday.

'My husband has told the police nothing of our arrangement,' María went on. 'It is just between us.'

'OK, I'll buy that for now,' he conceded, 'but I'll be taking precautions. So let's get this over as soon as possible. Hanging about makes me nervous.'

Holliday prepared the *Ellabella* to sail. The rendezvous had been set. He weighed anchor and set the course.

He began taking his precautions. He had three MAK 10 machine pistols on board. His, and the two dead blacks'. Also three Glock handguns.

The Big Macs, as the machine pistols were known, he placed fully loaded at strategic positions in the band of his shorts and concealed the other two around the boat.

He had chosen darkness to make the handover. It just seemed a good idea. With all the prep done, he took the boat off automatic and steered it himself for a while. It gave him time to think.

The afternoon shaded to evening. The evening darkened to night. He was almost there. He could hear the breakers crashing onto the rocks. He cut the engine and dropped anchor into shallow water.

He fetched the women from inside the boat.

'A final farewell drink together,' he told them.

Fifty-one

Jesús Alcantara spoke with José Miguel Gallega over the phone. Señor Gallega agreed that he would willingly pay the 2 million euros if it were necessary.

His wife's safety was paramount.

However, as Jesús pointed out, when dealing with these sorts of people you nearly always ended up with no money and most of the time a body.

No witnesses!

The kidnapper, now hero-cum-rescuer, was only one man. Jesús Alcantara was Spanish Special Forces. Liam Dooley was... God only knows. Kevin Goulding was a cool, merciless killer, no doubt about that.

Surely the three of them could deal with one man. Señor Gallega agreed to let Jesús Alcantara deal with the situation as it unfolded.

And he would send the cash immediately.

On board the thirty-foot cabin cruiser *La Diversión* – ('Fun' in English) – Jesús, Dooley and Goulding made plans.

'He'll be nervous, for sure,' Dooley said, stating the obvious. 'That makes him dangerous and unpredictable.'

Kevin Goulding was licking the paper of his roll-up. 'Well, I say youse two keep him calm and talking, and at the first chance I get I'll blow his fucking head off.'

'Good man yerself,' Dooley congratulated him. 'As ever, a real forward thinker. I couldn't have put it better meself.'

Jesús Alcantara appealed for calm. 'Amigos, please! We have to think of the señoras' safety as paramount.'

'Well, if the eejit's got no head I can't think of anything more paramount than that,' said Goulding. 'Whatever it fuckin' means.'

'Amigos, amigos, *please*. Nothing must happen to the señoras,' Jesús pleaded. 'We must do nothing to endanger them.'

It was Dooley's turn next. 'I'm sorry, auld son, but there's always got to be a risk. We just have to stay ahead of the game.'

Jesús tried to get control.

'It will be dark when we rendezvous. His choice. So he has to think it an advantage. But it can also work for us.'

'Well,' Goulding concluded, 'there's only so much talking you can do. In the end it comes down to what happens at the time. If I keep out of sight I've got a clear shot at him, sometime. And believe me, I only need one.

The time was coming.

It was almost midnight. There was a half-moon with a clear sky and the stars twinkled.

On the *Ellabella*, Doc Holliday had cuffed the two women's ankles to each other. A second set of handcuffs held Sonia Carabantes to the rail of the boat by her wrist.

They weren't going swimming.

Holliday started his engine. He manoeuvred the boat to a seaward position and raised the anchor.

He was ready to take off, if needs be...

The two boats converged on each other. Holliday stood behind the women. Only Dooley and Jesús could be seen on deck.

Dooley called across the water, 'God bless all here tonight.'

'Cut the crap!' snarled Holliday. 'Got the money?'

' 'Tis a pagan, you are,' moaned Dooley, hurt.

'I might be a pagan but I ain't a cunt. So don't fuck this thing up, or you'll have two dead women on your hands.'

Jesús Alcantara tried to cool it. 'There is no need for, how you say, a fuck-up, amigo. We are all men of the world. We are all professionals here to do a trade.'

'Fair enough,' said Holliday calmly, 'so here's the deal. You cruise slowly by the *Ellabella* and toss the money onto the deck and keep going. I'll check it, and if it's all OK you can cruise around again and pick up the women.'

'Amigo!' Jesús began to protest.

'Take it or leave it. That's the deal.'

Holliday picked up the MAK 10 from the deck and shielded himself behind the women.

'Now, slowly, past.'

La Diversión adjusted itself and slowly moved alongside the *Ellabella*. Jesús Alcantara tossed a holdall over onto the deck. Holliday was like a cat. His eyes flicked everywhere.

But it was his nose that alerted him. Neither of the two men on the boat was smoking. But he could smell cigarette smoke. Then he saw something glow in the dark from behind the main wheelhouse. There was a flash of flame and a burning pain as a bullet tore through his ear.

Then all hell broke loose.

Holliday emptied the MAK 10 at the direction of the shot. Bullets shattered wood and smashed glass. He heard an agonising scream of death as Goulding ruptured in floods of blood onto the deck.

Dooley and Jesús fired simultaneously, but Holliday had thrown himself to the deck. The women did the same for cover. Holliday crawled furiously to his second MAK 10. He snatched it up and fired over the rail at the *La Diversión*. As it passed by the *Ellabella*, the devastation caused by the automatic weapon was appalling.

For good measure, running at a crouch, Holliday went for the third MAK 10.

Standing up tall, he rained fire onto the retreating boat.

Everything on the deck was destroyed.

'Fuckin' cunts!' he screamed as he threw the gun to the deck.

Fifty-two

Holliday gunned the engine of the *Ellabella* and took off.

He didn't think anyone would be following. The women cowered on the deck, cuffed together. Sonia's wrist was bleeding where she hung from the rail.

'Unlock me, please,' she pleaded.

'When I got time.'

'I'm in pain.'

'And what the fuck do you think I'm in? Half my fucking ear is blown off!'

'I'm sorry.'

'Forget it.'

'I'll fix it. I can do first aid.'

'Thanks.'

'*De nada.*'

After an hour out to sea, when he felt safe, Holliday stopped the boat.

'I'm sorry about all this,' he apologised. 'It wasn't my fault.'

'I know,' said María Luisa Gallega. 'It is very regrettable. I don't know what went wrong.'

'Well, something did, for sure,' said Holliday. 'Perhaps it was just a breakdown in communication.'

He laughed, and even the two women couldn't help a smile.'

'Yes. I'm sure that was all it was,' agreed Sonia Carabantes. 'So if you can free us, perhaps we can all help each other.'

'Sure. I don't suppose you've seen my ear anywhere?'

Kevin Goulding was dead.

Liam Dooley had a gaping hole in his shoulder, and still felt he was lucky. Jesús Alcantara was shot in the left thigh. But no bones were broken and the main arteries had been missed, so he felt lucky too.

La Diversión looked anything but...

The owners whom they'd rented it from... Well, it might be better to just scuttle her and save the explanations.

'Jesus, Mary and Joseph!' cried Dooley. 'If ever there was a right fuck-up, then this was it. That was more fire power than I ever saw in Belfast. And poor Kevin there, cut to pieces.'

Jesús Alcantara was in despair. 'I don't know how I'm ever going to explain this to Señor Gallega.'

'And losing the money too.'

'Please! No more.'

'Well, auld son, we need patching up – and a drink. It's way past midnight.'

'On that I'll certainly agree.'

On the *Ellabella*, Sonia Carabantes admired the bandage on Doc Holliday's head. 'I think, señor, if you grow your hair you won't even notice it.'

'Great. Cheers!'

'It is very fashionable in Spain.'

'So what happens to us now?' María asked. 'I fear for us.'

'Well, it sure got worse rather than better.'

'*Sí, señor*. I know.'

'We'll talk about it in the morning. But for now, I think we could all do with a drink.'

He was definitely getting too used to the drink, he thought.

But it should dull the pain.

Shouldn't it?

Fifty-three

I was shaking with rage and emotion. On top of the grief, it was almost unbearable.

The bastard had phoned me. I had spoken to him.

It had to be him.

How else could he have known about McGouldrick?

McGouldrick. Sitting next to me.

Through tears of grief, rage and anger, I told him what had just happened.

The bastard had phoned me.

I still couldn't quite believe it.

'Tomorrow, Jack,' seethed McGouldrick. 'First thing. We must get to Antequera. It all starts there. We'll find him.'

It was barely light in the morning when we were on our way. We took clothes and weapons and anything we needed and piled it in the boot of the Jaguar soft top. We ate up the miles and it was barely waking up time when we drew up across the road from the café I had read about in the paper.

The one where Esther Fernandez had met her killer.

It was closed.

I was in despair – not because the café was closed, but because I didn't share McGouldrick's optimism. I just couldn't see what we were going to achieve.

In my opinion the killer was long gone. I said so.

'Jack, I'm disappointed in ye,' he told me. 'Yer not thinking straight. How did he get here? How did he get away? He had to have a car, or he had to get on a bus or train. We have to find out. He must have stayed somewhere. Who did he speak to? What did he say? What can they remember? We have to dig away.'

He was right, of course. I had to get more positive. I could see it now: McGouldrick was the oasis of optimism and I was the desert of pessimism.

I snapped out of it.

'Good,' declared McGouldrick.

The café was opening. We left the Jaguar and took a table on the pavement. Almost instantly, the waiter appeared at our table. We ordered the local special breakfast that included scrambled eggs and fresh bread, fruit and coffee. We were the only people in the café, so I asked. 'Esther Fernandez, did you know her?'

Somewhat surprised, he said, 'Of course, señor. She was a local señorita – a tour guide for our town. She was very popular. But why do you ask?'

'She was murdered by the same man who murdered my girlfriend,' I told him. 'I want to find him.'

'Of course, señor.'

He sat down at our table.

'He is a very bad man, señor. He needs to be caught.'

'And we intend to catch him, auld son,' said McGouldrick.

'Of course, and for sure I will do everything I can to help you. But what? The police are doing everything they can.'

'Esther Fernandez spent two hours with a man here in your café during the day she was killed,' I told him. 'Is there anything you can remember about him?' I stressed the question. 'No matter how small. Anything.'

'He was very charming, señor, for sure.' The waiter went on, 'Polite, well mannered, a real gentleman. He ordered a bottle of white wine for himself. When he was joined by Esther Fernandez she had a cappuccino. She had none of the wine but the bottle was empty when they left.'

'Is that unusual?' I asked.

'I thought it was a lot when one is driving, señor,' the waiter replied.

'How do you know he was driving?' I asked.

'The car was parked right outside, señor.'

'What car was it?' I asked.

'A hired Seat, señor.'

'How do you know it was hired?'

'The plates, the stickers. It was hired from Record out of Malaga Airport. And señor, his first name is David. I heard them introduce themselves to one another.'

'*Gracias, señor*,' I thanked him. 'You have been a great help.'

'*De nada, señor.*'

'So what did I tell you?' crowed McGouldrick, 'And we haven't even had breakfast!'

It was a good result.

I phoned Sebastian Aparicio.

He was on the case.

It was then he told me about the disaster with Jesús.

And Kevin Goulding getting killed.

I told McGouldrick.

He stopped eating.

'KG knew the risks,' he said. 'I've seen many a good man fall. And to be sure he was one of the best. He'll be missed. But as they say in Ireland, when the rain has fallen, there's no way you can put it back in the sky.'

He summoned the waiter over. 'Two San Miguels, auld son, and *gracias*. It's a breakfast drink we'll be havin' for Kevin. And God rest his soul... if he had one, of course.'

The second thing we knew for certain about Esther Fernandez' movements the day that she died was the name of the restaurant she ate in. It wasn't open for business when we got there but there was a lot of activity inside. The door was open so we walked in.

'The restaurant is closed, I'm afraid, señor,' the waiter told me.

'Yes, I'm sorry,' I said, 'but we haven't come to eat.'

I explained.

'Yes, señor, I remember them well,' the head waiter told me. 'I served them myself.'

'Is there anything you can remember about them?' I asked.

'We serve many people, señor.' After giving me the descriptions of them that I already had, he said, 'The 1966 Sandeman vintage port. The very best and most expensive. Exquisite. I remember that.'

'Well, that clinches it,' announced McGouldrick. 'It's definitely the same boyo.'

'Now all we have to do is find him,' I said.

Fifty-four

Doc Holliday had a splitting headache. Not surprising, really. He was lucky to have a head at all. This whole thing was getting more bizarre all the time.

After a few drinks they'd slept for a few hours, and now a new day had begun. It was warming up nicely – as usual, another perfect day on the Costa del Sol.

Sonia was cooking omelettes. Spanish, of course. Holliday was trying to work out what would happen next. And he still couldn't believe that he had the 2 million euros. They'd actually thrown him the real money.

Bizarre!

'How's the head?' María asked him.

'Pounding.'

Is there anything I can do?'

'There is, actually.'

It had been creeping up slowly on María Luisa Gallega. The feelings. Every hour, every conversation, every drink, she found herself feeling more and more drawn to Holliday. She was beginning to think of him in the night. She thought a lot about his fit body. His manhood, that she had so easily relieved for him. His good humour. And he was a real man, not like her husband.

She wanted to kiss him.

She wanted it badly.

For a second their eyes fixed together.

'Fancy a swim?' Holliday asked.

'I do, but your ear...'

'Just don't knock the bandage off.'

'Very well, señor.'

They undressed purposefully and slowly. María dived naked into the sea. Holliday lowered himself slowly into the water. He was hard already when María, treading water, put her arms around his neck and sucked for all she was worth onto his willing mouth.

They clawed and pawed and kissed and bit. She held his. He fingered hers. They sank in the water and surfaced, gasping.

'This is no good,' coughed Holliday. 'Let's get back on the boat.'

'Sí.'

They climbed back onto the deck.

María said to Sonia, 'I do what I must do to save us. Can you go below, please?'

Sonia noticed the Doc's six inches of throbbing muscle. 'I can see that, María. Thank you for your sacrifice. I'm sure you will be rewarded.'

She went below.

Holliday kissed María with a passion he had never felt before in his whole life. Maybe it was the Spanish thing... different. Or maybe it was María. She was special.

She hungered for him.

Devouring him.

She dropped to her knees and took him into her mouth. He threw his throbbing head back and groaned in ecstasy. He stopped her just seconds away from the magic moment.

Holliday wanted her to share fully in the pleasure. Not that that seemed to be a problem. He raised her to her feet and they kissed again violently.

Still in the throes of passion, they sidestepped to the boat rail. Kissing and biting, María sat on the rail, holding on with both hands. As he leaned back, Holliday penetrated deeply into her, holding himself back until the last second when he felt her orgasm coming. Together they cried out as she gripped the rails and he crushed the breath from her.

Slowly they regained their breath and, sliding off the rail, they folded into each other's arms.

Sonia Carabantes said from behind them, 'I don't know how to thank you, María. If that cannot save us, then nothing ever can.'

Fifty-five

The walking wounded, Jesús Alcantara and Liam Dooley, had patched each other up. They wrapped Kevin Goulding in some old tarpaulin they found, along with anything heavy that they could find. They tied the parcel up well and threw it into the sea. Dooley said a few disinterested words. Jesús made the sign of the cross.

'Jesus, this is a find old mess,' he said, stating the obvious.

Jesús Alcantara sighed deeply. 'What am I going to say to Señor Gallega?'

'May I suggest, auld son, that you are a little economical with the truth. As I remember it, he fired first.'

'*Claro.*'

'I never saw Goulding fire. Did you?'

'No.'

'So he must have fired first.'

'For sure.'

'There you go then.'

Jesús Alcantara made his call.

When it was over, he said to Dooley, 'We can never return the boat in this condition. There would simply be too many questions to answer.'

'I hear what you're saying on that one,' agreed Dooley. 'Let's get close to shore and sink her. I'll inflate the life raft.'

Sonia Carabantes and María Luisa Gallega were drinking cava and giggling like two little schoolgirls. It was mid-afternoon, and both were enhancing their all-over tan. As was Doc Holliday.

After rebandaging his ear, Sonia had declared that it looked well. As she was inspecting it closely she accidentally brushed her breasts across his face.

'You'll be fine, señor,' she declared. 'It is clean and infection-free. It will heal very well.'

'Thanks,' he said, slightly distracted by the closeness of her naked body. He could feel the warmth of it.

'You're welcome.'

As the two women giggled, Doc took more pain killers with his sixth San Miguel of the afternoon.

And tried to figure things out.

Maybe it was the headache or maybe the distraction of the two beautiful women, but he just couldn't think straight. The passion he had shared with María was amazing and he genuinely had feelings for her. But that fleeting moment when Sonia had accidentally brushed her breasts against his face confused him...

He couldn't help feeling how good it might be to have a threesome.

And to be honest, he didn't feel it would be out of the question.

And he had the money.

He could just let them go and he could disappear.

But for some reason he didn't want to do that.

Well, he couldn't be arsed with it all now.

He opened his seventh San Miguel of the afternoon.

Fifty-six

Sebastian Aparicio rode his police motorcycle into the dark basement car park at Malaga Airport. He illegally parked outside the Record Renta-Car desk, where there were four busy clerks.

Not standing in a line to wait his turn, he went to the front.

'Señorita, please. I need to talk to you. This is urgent police business.'

'Of course, señor.'

The girl apologised to the customer returning a car. She would be right back. The customer looked none too pleased. He had a plane to catch. Sebastian told the customer to step back. He looked even more displeased. A threatening look, and he stepped back.

'How can I help you?' the girl asked.

'I would like you to check your computer records for me and try to find a man you rented a medium-sized Seat to.'

'When?'

'I don't know.'

'But…'

'Try within the last two weeks.'

'But señor, what am I looking for? Look at all these people! We rent many cars.'

'I'm certain he is English.'

She spread her hands. 'So?'

'I am beginning to find you obstructive, señorita. This is a murder inquiry. If I have to I will close your offices and bring in my own people to check your records. So what is it to be?'

'Give me a clue.'

'His first name is David.'

She worked the computer.

'In the last two weeks there are eight Davids. Colour of car?'

'Not sure.'

'Red?'

'No.'

'White?'

'No.'

'Blue?'

'No.'

'Metallic?'

'Yes. But I don't know the exact colour.'

'Four cars. Do you have a description of the man?'

Sebastian told her what he knew.

The señorita smiled. 'Yes, I remember him. A real ladies' man. Charming. He flirted outrageously with me. He was very attractive and smartly dressed. He said he looked forward greatly to returning the car, and hoped I would be the one to deal with him. He shook my hand and kissed it. He couldn't possibly be a killer.'

'I believe he is, señorita.'

She punched the keys.

'David Walker. Indefinite rental.'

She pressed another key.

She handed Sebastian an enlarged photo of David Walker taken from his driving licence.

'Now can I get on with my work?'

It was 45 km from Malaga to Antequera.

Police motorcyclist Sebastian Aparicio did it in just over half an hour, siren and lights blaring.

I was sitting with Johnny McGouldrick outside the pavement café where Esther Fernandez had met David Walker. I was drinking a large beer, McGouldrick was drinking a small beer. And a large Bushmills.

Sebastian stopped at the kerb beside us and dismounted from his bike. He called the waiter.

'*Una cerveza, per favor!*'

He sat with us and thrust into my hand the printout.

'David Walker.'

The waiter brought the beer. I gave him the picture.

'*Sí, señor.* That is the man who sat here with Esther Fernandez.'

'*Gracias.*'

Sebastian was excited. 'When I pass this on to headquarters they are sure to collect him in hours.'

Johnny McGouldrick was smoking a medium-size cheap Spanish cigar.

'And do what with him?' he asked.

'Arrest him, of course.'

'And what?'

'Put him in prison, of course.'

'Not good enough, auld son. I want him for myself.'

Fifty-seven

David Walker had enjoyed taunting Jack.

In fact he was laughing.

He'd used a public phone, of course. He wasn't stupid.

But now he had to move on. To Córdoba.

182 km from Malaga, Córdoba has had a glorious past. Under the Moors it became Western Europe's biggest, most cultured city. Packed with monuments and echoes of the past, but in its own way living vibrantly, today it is a city which leaves an indelible mark in the memory.

Most of Córdoba sits on the Rio Guadalquivir's northern bank, with mountains not far behind. It is the capital of a province whose variety and interest are being discovered by an increasing number of visitors.

Thanks to expectations of a deluge of visitors spilling over from Expo '92 in Seville, Córdoba has a number of quiet new hotels. Including Parador Nacional de la Arruzafa, a four star hotel with big rooms, gardens and pool in a quiet residential area.

It was here that David Walker decided to stay.

After inspecting his room and unpacking his bag he decided on a drink by the pool. He ordered a bottle of his favourite cava, Freixenet. It came to him beautifully presented in an ice bucket with a crisp white towel over the top. The waiter set down two Freixenet flutes and filled just one, as David Walker had asked.

As he sipped at the wine in the shade of his table umbrella, he was searching out a potential victim.

The voices in his head were demanding another kill.

It was too soon, though.

He knew that.

Too risky.

But how could he stop?

He was no longer the one in control.

So who *was* in control?

It must be the other fucker!

The one in his head!

There were potential victims everywhere. But how did you choose one? Or did they just choose themselves?

'Hi,' said Jane, the Thompsons hotel rep. 'Are you with Thompsons?'

'I'm not with anyone.' David Walker smiled at her. She was a real looker: blonde, slim and tanned, with a warm, friendly smile.

'You're obviously expecting somebody,' she remarked, eyeing up the second glass and winking.

'I'm afraid not,' he replied, and added a little sadly, 'just living in hope.' Then thoughtfully, 'Perhaps you could fulfil my hopes?'

'Perhaps I could at that,' she said sitting down opposite him.

He filled the second empty glass. My name is David,' he told her. 'I can see by your badge that you are Jane Thompsons.'

'No,' she corrected him. 'Jane, yes; Thompsons, no. That's who I work for.'

He laughed. 'Yes, I know. I was joking.'

Jane laughed too. 'You're winding me up, yes?'

'Yes.'

She was liking him already.

'So how long have you been here, Jane?' he asked.

'Third season.' She smiled easily. 'I love it. So what do you do? You know what I do.'

'I'm a writer,' he replied, which wasn't really too far from the truth.

'What do you write?'

'Books, TV plays, some songs, magazine articles,' he said, shrugging his shoulders. 'Anything really.'

'How wonderful and interesting… I'd love to do that.'

'Anyone can do it.'

'I doubt that. A lot of people might think they can do it, but I don't think there are many who can.'

Modestly, he said, 'Well, perhaps. Anyway, I'd rather talk about you. What time do you finish tonight?'

'God! You don't waste much time.'

'Time is too precious to waste.'

'After the welcome meeting.'

142

'What time is that?'

'If I don't get any prats asking stupid questions, about 8.30.'

'So I'll book a table for ten o'clock and meet you in the bar at 9.30. We can walk to the restaurant.'

'Hold on! There's fast and there's fast! What restaurant?'

'El Churrasco.'

'*El Churrasco*!' Jane gasped. 'Have you any idea how expensive it is?'

'I haven't got a clue,' David Walker confessed, 'and quite frankly I couldn't care less. As my grandfather always told me, "Son, you only live once. And if you do it right, once is enough." '

Sebastian Aparicio's contacts in the Police Force were checking all the computer updates on the passports presented in hotels by guests checking in.

It was late in the evening when he received a call telling him that David Walker had registered at Hotel Parador Nacional de la Arruzafa in Córdoba.

It was nearly 10.15 when we started the dash to Córdoba. Well over the drink-drive limit, I drove myself and Johnny McGouldrick in the open-top Jaguar.

With the police motorcycle escort leading.

At 11 p.m. we were outside David Walker's hotel.

Sebastian was quickly carrying out his investigations.

The receptionist at the hotel had called the restaurant and handed the phone to David Walker. He had requested the best table in the restaurant and also asked if they stocked 1966 Sandeman vintage port.

They didn't. But they would get some, and would have it decanted for him and ready for his cheese and biscuits.

It was expensive, and he agreed to pay for the whole bottle.

The head waiter met them in the restaurant reception area. David Walker gave him fifty euros.

'Only the best, please.'

'Of course, señor.'

And so the tone of the evening was set.

The chase was on.

The build-up to the kill.

As El Churrasco was known for its grilled meals, David and Jane chose swordfish steaks. David had gone for the Freixenet again. It was perfect with the swordfish.

The exquisitely wonderful port completed the evening. Jane had been transfixed from the beginning with David's charm, charisma and witty conversation.

She had already decided that if he suggested it she would sleep with him.

How could she resist? After all, he was a man to die for...

We knew from Sebastian's enquiries where they had gone. We also knew the address of the small apartment block that Jane, the hotel's Thompson representative, lived in.

When we got to the restaurant the head waiter told us that they had left together about fifteen minutes earlier.

We had to dash.

Fifty-eight

It was evening again on the *Ellabella*. The smell of cooking filled the air.

Garlic. Lots of it.

Sonia Carabantes could cook! And drink. She seemed only to cook with a bottle of red wine. María Luisa Gallega preferred white. Doc Holliday was staying with San Miguel. Sitting, bottle in hand, opposite María, he said, 'Phone your husband,' and handed her his cell phone. 'I want to talk to him.'

She made the call. 'José, it is I. Yes, I am well. Do not worry, I have not been harmed. But no thanks to you. You almost got me killed! Mr Holliday wishes to speak with you.'

She passed the phone.

'Mr Gallega, I have no wish to harm your wife. I have done everything to ensure her safety. I have killed two men who threatened her. Then, when I am trying to give her back to you, somebody shoots my ear off and almost kills your wife and her friend! What was all that about?'

On the other end of the line, José Miguel Gallega said, 'I am sorry, señor. That was nothing to do with me. The work of fools, is all I can say. I want my wife back. What must I do?'

'I will only deal with you from now on, Mr Gallega,' Holliday replied. 'I want nothing more than the safe return of your wife unharmed. No more fools. I have my reward. I want nothing more than your assurance as a gentleman that when I bring her back to you that will be the end of the matter.'

'I assure you, señor, on my word of honour. It shall be so.'

'Then speak to your wife, and she will confirm that I have been nothing but a gentleman towards her.'

He passed the phone back to María. She spoke for a time then passed the cell phone back.

Señor Gallega spoke again. 'In two days' time I am delivering my finest fighting bull to the ring in Córdoba. He is to fight the finest bullfighter in all Spain: José Tomas. It would be wonderful if you could bring my wife to the bullfight. You could be my guest of honour. It would also show the world and the police your sincerity. You will be the hero of all Spain. And a free man.'

'You've talked me into it.'

La Diversión was sunk.

Jesús Alcantara and Liam Dooley were washing up on the beach in the inflatable.

Still bloody and wounded, they scrambled out and dragged it onto the beach. In the early hours of the morning, the Carihuela beach in Torremolinos was deserted. There were showers on the beach. They used them to clean up, then changed into the clean clothes they had brought with them. They sat on a beach bed outside a closed up bar.

'Too bad the bar's shut,' said Dooley. 'Yer man didn't sound too happy, auld son.'

He was referring to the call Jesús Alcantara had made to José Miguel Gallega.

'You could hardly blame him, señor. He's handling the whole thing himself from now on.'

'Well, there goes me reward.'

'We might as well get the train in the morning and join Jack and McGouldrick.'

'Might be a long old night,' said Dooley. 'Do you think there's any chance the bar might open?'

Jesús Alcantara looked puzzled. 'The bar, open?'

Dooley found some tools for the outside barbecue and easily broke off the flimsy padlock on the beach bar.

'Bejasus,' he cried, 'it's a miracle!'

Fifty-nine

The *Ellabella* docked back in Puerto Duquesa.

'Ladies,' Holliday began, 'tonight will be our last night together. Let's make it a good one. We've been through a lot together. Some good, some bad.'

'*Sí.*'

'I know a hotel, not far from here. Beach Hotel Las Dunas. It's located between Estepona and Marbella. It's luxurious with a gourmet restaurant.'

'I've heard of it,' said Sonia Carabantes.

'So let's book *a* room, then go shopping to Marbella for new clothes and have the meal of a lifetime in their restaurant.'

'You said book a room,' said María Luisa Gallega.

'Well, it's a very expensive hotel,' said Holliday, 'and I'm sure as it's our very last night ever we'd want to be all together. That's all!'

A grin crept across the face of Sonia Carabantes. After all, she had *seen* what she was missing. And her friend María Luisa Gallega *knew* what she was missing.

And Sonia knew that María knew, that she knew, that Sonia knew what she was missing...

They all knew!

God, life's so confusing!

The hotel was amazing. The room was huge. The receptionist eyed them suspiciously. A family room? They didn't look much like a family.

Taking a taxi to Marbella, they shopped for hours and then took a taxi back. Holliday ordered cava to the room and a few nibbles for the afternoon.

They sat on the balcony in the afternoon sun.

'I feel somehow sad,' María announced. 'I think I will miss you.'

'It's strange the way things turned out,' said Holliday wistfully. 'I mean, we're friends.'

'And lovers too,' chipped in Sonia. 'Well, not all of us – yet!'

'From this moment to Córdoba,' said María, 'let's make this the greatest day of our life. We must all swear that what happens now until then will never be spoken of again.'

'I swear,' said Sonia.

'I definitely swear,' said Holliday.

'Then so it is done,' concluded María, pouring cava into three flutes.

The farewell party began.

Calmly at first. They reminisced over the day's events and soon the cava was gone. Another quickly arrived. Chatting, snacking and drinking, they were barely aware that the time had slipped away until Holliday yawned. 'I think we should have a sleep and be fresh for dinner.'

'*Sí, con mucho gusto,*' the two señoras agreed.

In the bedroom, without ceremony all three undressed and climbed into the king-sized bed.

Sandwiched between the two naked women, Holliday first leaned over and kissed María. He then leaned the other way and kissed Sonia. At this time passion was not on the menu.

But when the two señoras leaned over him and passionately kissed each other, he started to feel a little excited.

It was dusk when they woke. They showered, dressed and went down to the bar. There was an air of expectation over the evening. They had cocktails in the bar: pina coladas.

In the restaurant, the flame-grilled king prawns were delicious. The fillet steak in garlic sauce was perfect, with cheese and pineapple and Bailey's Irish Cream.

In some sort of an animated state, each one of them contemplated what was to come. When they moved back to the bar, a bottle of cava in ice was on a table for them.

'I've never been to Córdoba,' confessed Holliday.

'It is magnificent,' said Sonia proudly. 'The bullring is one of the best in Spain.'

'My husband is bringing his very best bull,' said María. 'Half a ton of fearless muscle. The torero, José Tomas, is Spain's highest paid.'

'I've never been to a bullfight,' Holliday owned up.

'Well, you couldn't have picked a better one to start with,' María declared. 'My husband breeds the finest bulls in Spain. With the best bull and the best torero, it has to be a spectacle.'

'I'm looking forward to it.'

'And as my husband's honoured guest, you will find it even more spectacular. And as the rescuer of his wife you may even be honoured.'

She was obviously proud of her husband, despite the fact that she was prepared to have the arse shagged off her tonight, he thought.

'I think we could finish this in the room. Don't you?' Holliday asked, picking up the ice bucket.

'Sí.'

Back in the room, a combination of lust, alcohol and the knowledge that this would be their last night alone together took over.

They tore off each other's clothes and everybody was kissing everybody. Holliday didn't seem to know which way to go, so he went with the flow. María and Sonia seemed content with each other. Holliday felt like a sideshow.

Never mind, though.

Arms, legs, boobs, everything seemed twisted in every direction. At first Holliday fretted about pleasing the women. Then it seemed perfectly obvious that they were OK on their own.

Eagerly trying to please all three of them, María sat on his face and Sonia impaled herself onto him.

While they both snogged each other passionately. Then, like an earthquake, he felt it coming. He thrust deeper and harder into Sonia Carabantes and pushed his face into María Luisa Gallega.

Then it was over, and they knew. They moved off him and continued on their own.

Sixty

We were fifteen minutes behind David Walker.

It was only a guess, and I hoped it was the right one, that they would go to Jane's place. That's where we went. Johnny McGouldrick seemed more eager than me.

He'd only met Barbara once. But in that one time he'd appreciated the wonderful gift that she was. I loved her with all of my heart. He knew that. Grief consumed me, though I tried not to show it.

Why? I don't know.

But McGouldrick knew too that he was partly responsible. If he hadn't flirted outrageously with Barbara I wouldn't have got pissed off enough to piss Barbara off.

And she had died a wicked and terrible death because of it all.

I was bent on revenge.

McGouldrick was bent on a *terrible* revenge. Revenge to him had been a way of life in Belfast.

God help David Walker if ever we found him...

As we rushed to Jane's address I thought about the call earlier from Jesús Alcantara and Liam Dooley. They were on their way to Córdoba, having failed to get the señoras back.

Soon we would be four.

As David Walker and Jane left the restaurant he slipped his arm around her waist. Tenderly. They stopped for a moment and looked at each other.

'I like you a lot,' said David. 'I've had a wonderful evening.'

'I have too,' Jane agreed, and kissed him gently and fleetingly.

They walked on slowly.

'My car is at the hotel,' said David. 'Would you like to go for a drive? I love the mountains at night. So marvellously beautiful and quiet. Peace itself.'

Completely under the spell of David Walker's charm, she said softly, 'I can't think of anything else I'd rather do at this moment.'

'Then we'll do it.'

They passed the Rio Guadalquivir's northern bank and on to the mountains not far behind. There was a bright three-quarter moon with a clear sky. David Walker found a beautiful place to park and stopped.

He felt for the small syringe and scalpel in his pocket.

They were there.

He slid his arm around Jane's neck and leaned over and kissed her.

She responded, and they kissed tenderly.

David Walker was happy.

But something wasn't normal.

Or was it?

He didn't know.

Because what was fucking normal?

He kissed Jane again.

'It's so beautiful here,' she said resting her head into his shoulders. 'I have the day off tomorrow and the greatest bullfighter in Spain, José Tomas, is to fight a great bull in the ring at Córdoba. It will be fantastic. Would you like to go? I can get us in for nothing.'

'I would like that a lot,' David Walker told her tenderly.

David Walker was a good man. He knew that. He wasn't a rapist. He wasn't a killer. He didn't track down women and brutally murder them.

Did he?

It was the other fucker!

The one in his head.

But how could he get rid of him?

That evil bastard that turned him into a monster.

But tonight at least he was David Walker.

A gentleman.

Jane had already decided she would have sex with David if he asked for it.

He didn't. He was a gentleman.

But they did kiss a lot and made plans for the bullfight the next day. And laughed.

We found the apartment and, fearing the worst when we got no answer, we broke in. There was nobody home.

With absolutely no authority we searched the apartment. Like burglars.

There was no sign of violence. No blood, no body.

'Maybe he took her back to his hotel,' I said.

'Not if he was going to kill her,' McGouldrick countered. 'That would be crazy.'

'He is crazy.'

'Not stupid, though.'

'I'm afraid I fear the worst.'

Sixty-one

The all-night beach party was over.

And what a party!

The sun rose early on the Costa del Sol. It was six in the morning and already warm.

'I think we should be gone, señor,' said Jesús Alcantara. 'I will leave some money for the drink and damage.'

'Why?' asked Liam Dooley incredulously.

'Because I have my honour, señor,' he responded, 'and am not a thief.'

Dooley shrugged. 'Fair enough, auld son.'

At the train station they examined the timetable and discovered that they were just in time for the first train of the day to Córdoba.

They phoned me to say they were on their way and could I meet them.

★

The atmosphere in the room at the Hotel Las Dunas was a little subdued.

After the wonderful day before that they had all had, they knew that the adventure was coming to an end.

From a kidnapping, to a friendship, to a rescue and reward, it was all very sad that they all knew that they could never be together like this again.

Perhaps it was best that way.

Sometimes life can be like a book. Full of chapters. You finish one then you start another one. Then you get to the end of the book. Then you read another.

There's no point in reading the same book twice. Not when there are so many others.

Well, it sounds easy!

'I feel so sad, Doc,' sighed María, 'and I can't bear to think of you never to be in my life again. I will miss you.'

'Don't start getting soppy on me,' said Holliday. 'I did kidnap you, after all. I might even have killed you!'

'Please do not talk such rubbish,' scolded Sonia Carabantes. 'You know that is not true.'

'Well… yes, but…'

'You know it is untrue, so don't say it.'

'OK,' he apologised. 'I'm sorry.'

'My husband cannot meet us himself at the train,' María informed Holliday. 'It is a hugely important day for him at the bullring. He will send a limousine to take us to our hotel. Then when we are ready we will be taken to the arena to meet him. The media will be there, in force. It will be a circus. I must remind you of our pact concerning our ordeal. You remember?'

'I remember,' Holliday confirmed. 'You can trust me on that.'

'Then kiss me, Doc, for the last time. I will miss you.'

'Me too.'

They embraced and kissed passionately.

Then Sonia Carabantes said, 'I also will miss you, Doc. A lot. In mind and spirit, you will always be my friend. Kiss me too, for the last time, and then we must go. To our future. But we'll kiss to the past.'

And they went.

Sixty-two

They were all in Córdoba now.

Jesús Alcantara and Liam Dooley. Shot up, but still walking.

María Luisa Gallega, Sonia Carabantes and the hero of the hour, Doc Holliday.

José Miguel Gallega was there with his bull. The best in all of Spain.

And I was there with Johnny McGouldrick.

And so was Jane with David Walker – and the fucked-up monster in his head.

Also there was José Tomas, the greatest bullfighter in the world.

And a sold-out show at the bullring in Córdoba.

After being picked up from the train station and taken to their hotel, María, Sonia and Doc had a drink. Then they went to their 'separate' rooms. An hour later they were back in the limo in their finest clothes on the way to the bullring.

'Remember our pact,' said María nervously.

The privacy screen was closed in the limo. Doc gripped María's forearm. 'I swear on my life. Trust me.'

She relaxed.

As the limo drew to a stop outside the VIP entrance to the ring, a posse of photographers, reporters and TV crews descended on the car.

Police cleared them back.

The chauffer stepped out and opened the door. María Luisa Gallega stepped out and waved to the crowd like a Hollywood star at the Oscars.

Her husband blended into her arms and they hugged for the television crews. Then Holliday stepped out and the crowd went mad, erupting into applause. He smiled and smiled. Cameras flashed. Microphones were thrust into his face. Question followed question.

He appealed for calm.

The mob quietened.

Had he really killed two black gangsters trying to rape Señora Gallega?

Yes, he had.

But raising his hands for quiet, he said, 'I don't think I did anything that any hero wouldn't do.'

The crowd went crazy.

I watched it on the television with McGouldrick, Dooley, Jesús and Sebastian.

Dooley drew in the roll-up fag he had just built. 'It might be me, but he shot the fuck out of us, killed Kevin, kidnapped two women and killed two of his own gang – and now he's a national hero. How does that work?'

'I don't know,' I said despairingly, 'but now that the Spanish women are safe I want to concentrate on finding the bastard who killed Barbara. And I'm worried sick about the Thompson's rep, Jane. Where is she? And where's David Walker?'

Sebastian Aparicio said, 'My people are exploring every avenue. He has not been back to his hotel and his car is gone. It is the holiday rep's day off, so she is not expected at the hotel. She has not yet returned to the apartment that you broke into. A criminal offence...'

'Not much by my usual standards,' I joked.

'That is true, amigo,' Sebastian conceded.

'So what can we do?' I asked.

'At the moment, nothing,' Sebastian told me. 'We just have to be patient. He will surface sometime. But from our previous knowledge, I don't expect to see the girl again.'

Sixty-three

They stayed the whole night in the mountains, David and Jane. It was romantic, and they both enjoyed it.

'I've never done that before,' Jane confessed. 'What a lovely thing to wake up to!'

'Neither have I,' said David Walker. 'And I don't know if it's the mountain air, but I'm starving.'

'I know a few places that open early for the local workers,' Jane volunteered. 'We could go to one.'

'Sounds good to me. Just point the way.'

The café was already quite busy with leathery skinned builders and a variety of morning people. They chose to sit out. It was quieter and less crowded. The waiter came to the table and they ordered two breakfasts.

'I like it here,' David Walker declared, taking in the surrounding area.

'Yes,' agreed Jane. 'It's a nice quiet urbanisation. A local area. Not many tourists.'

There was a sign across the street outside a small apartment building: *Alquilar* (To Let).

'I think I'll take a look at that after breakfast.'

The apartment was one bed, a nice dining room, kitchen and bathroom. David Walker liked it. It was tastefully furnished and reasonably priced. He agreed a month's rental and paid for it. He was getting a little tired of hotels, and besides, it was a whole lot cheaper.

'Do you always act so impulsively?' asked Jane.

'Always.'

David drove her home. He dropped her outside as she handed him her cell phone number.

'Call me later.'

'I will. I'm looking forward to the bullfight.'

'Me too.'

He drove to his hotel, and in no time at all had checked out and gone.

To his new apartment.

A garage at the back came with the apartment. David Walker used it. The car would be cooler and he didn't intend to use it for a few days.

There was a small, well-stocked *supermercado* not far down the street. He stocked up for the week and sat on his balcony for a while with a brandy.

His head felt calm and he felt good.

He thought about Jane and how much he liked her.

How lucky she was to be alive!

He was so glad.

Meanwhile, Jane didn't realise her flat had been broken into, so expertly had it been done, the lock had been so cleanly picked and the door reclosed and nothing looked disturbed.

She showered and thought about David Walker and the bullfight that afternoon. When she answered the doorbell she was surprised to see me and a Spanish policeman in the doorway.

'*Hola, señorita*,' said Sebastian Aparicio. 'You are well?'

'Yes,' she replied, 'very well. Is there any reason why I shouldn't be?'

'May we come in, señorita?'

'Of course.'

'Where did you spend last night, señorita?'

'Why do you want to know? What business is it of yours?'

I left all the talking to Sebastian. He was the policeman, after all.

'We have reason to believe that David Walker, the man you may have spent the night with, is a psychopathic serial killer who has murdered brutally at least seven or eight women.'

'Absolute rubbish!' Jane protested. 'The man is a gentleman. You're crazy!'

I was getting really frustrated. I had to say something.

'The bastard murdered my girlfriend and a beautiful girl called Esther Fernandez. You must have seen it in the news.'

'I saw it all in the news, but I didn't see anything that said it was David.'

'Where did you spend the night?' demanded Sebastian.

'In the mountains in his car,' she answered. 'And he was a perfect gentleman.'

'So I keep hearing,' I snapped, 'But the bastard butchered my girlfriend.'

'What proof do you have?'

'He was the last person with her,' I countered.

'How do you know that?'

'He told me.'

'When?'

'He phoned me.'

'How do you know it was him?'

'I know.'

'So you saw him and have a written confession? He killed your girlfriend.'

'I don't have a written confession.'

'Then what do you have?'

Sebastian intervened. 'Please. Calm. You spent the night in his car. What then?'

'We went for breakfast and he dropped me back here and went to his hotel, Parador Nacional de la Arruzafa.'

'He checked out of there,' I said, almost accusingly. 'So where is he now?'

'How the hell should I know?' Jane snapped. 'Anywhere in Spain, for all I know. We only had dinner together. We're not married.'

'You don't know how lucky you are to be alive,' I told her.

'Says who? Now, why don't you just fuck off and leave me alone. I'm fine!'

Sixty-four

It was the most eagerly awaited bullfight in Spain for years: the great José Tomas against the best bull José Miguel Gallega could provide.

With his wife and Sonia Carabantes and the rescuing hero, Doc Holliday, they sat with the rest of the VIPs drinking champagne.

I was there with Johnny McGouldrick. Sebastian had taken Jesús Alcantara and Liam Dooley to a police doctor to have their wounds properly seen to.

David Walker had collected Jane in a taxi, and with Jane's contacts found themselves in one of the better positions in the arena.

The moment was coming…

I was looking forward to my first bullfight. I needed something to take my mind away from the terrible events of the last few days.

As I came out of the corridor to take my seat, I felt a sort of dizzy amusement. With McGouldrick next to me, I waited. Torrents of light flooded the arena and an immense rumble drifted up from the crowd. All eyes were fixed on the fateful door of the arena. I must admit that my heart was as tight as if squeezed by an invisible hand. My temples buzzed, and hot and cold perspiration ran up my back, one of the strangest emotions I have ever felt. A light fanfare rang out; two swinging doors were flung open, and the bull rushed into the middle of the arena, while an immense hurrah went up from the crowd. It was a superb animal, almost all black and shining, with a square muzzle, spindly legs, a tail always moving, sharp, crescent-shaped horns, and between his shoulders he wore a ruffle of ribbon with the colours of his *ganadería* stuck into the hide with a needle. He paused a moment, sniffing the air a few times, dazzled by the tumult. Then, spying the first picador, the bull set out after him with a furious thrust.

I was enthralled by it all, so was McGouldrick. Neither of us spoke a word.

The battle began – banderillas were placed on the beast, whose blood glistened on his coat.

The picadors withdrew, leaving the field open to José Tomas, who had gone to the *logia de ayuntamiento* to ask permission to kill the bull.

Permission granted, he threw his *montera* into the air as if to show he would give it his 'all' and walked with a deliberate step toward the bull, hiding his sword under the red folds of his muleta.

He flashed the red scarf several times, upon which the bull rushed blindly; a slight movement sufficed for José Tomas to avoid the thrust of the wild beast. It returned quickly to the charge, giving the red cloth furious blows with its head.

At this point it seemed that the bull tore up the script and rewrote it.

José Tomas, the undisputed David Beckham of Spanish bullfighting, a darling heart-throb with an adoring female following, suddenly found the raging half-ton bull getting the better of him.

The crowd were certainly getting their money's worth.

In dramatic style, the celebrity bullfighter was completely outfoxed by the bull, who tossed him into the air. After crashing to the ground, Tomas was skewered by the bull's ferocious horns, before being hurled skywards for the second time.

The crowd went wild. We all love the underdog...

Despite this being his second *cornada*, or goring, in under a month (he had been hospitalised after a bullfight in Jerez just two weeks before), the battered Tomas somehow managed to get back on his feet and kill the bull.

We were both breathless.

McGouldrick said, 'That was truly amazing.'

'I don't think a football match will ever quite be the same,' I replied.

In recognition of his extraordinary chutzpah, Tomas was rewarded with both ears and the tail of the bull, and was later carried out of the ring on a colleague's shoulders – the customary reward for feats of great bravery.

The poor brave bull was dragged away in a trail of blood through the sand to be butchered up.

Not very fair, really, I thought.

Sixty-five

The bullfight had been a short distraction from my grief for Barbara.

It was beginning to sink in.

The terrible way she had been butchered.

I had been so sure it was David Walker. Now I had doubts. Jane was alive and well and would listen to nothing bad about David Walker.

And I wasn't convinced that she knew nothing of his whereabouts.

'What evidence?' she'd asked.

I was confused.

I returned south to the farm with Johnny McGouldrick.

Sebastian was there with the patched up Liam Dooley and Jesús Alcantara. Sebastian informed me that David Walker had disappeared.

'He is no longer at the hotel and we cannot find his car. He may have gone to ground.'

McGouldrick said, 'He'll turn up. He has to eventually, and I'll be there to help the sinner repent.'

Dooley joined in. 'I could use a drink, auld son. We've a lot to talk about. This whole thing seems to have gone tits up.'

I couldn't argue with that. 'So what do you want to talk about?' I asked.

'Money, for a start,' he began, 'but let's sort the drinks out first.'

'I'm not waiting on you,' I told him. 'Help yourselves.'

Jesús, Sebastian and I had beer. The two Irishmen started a fresh bottle of Bushmills. We sat by the pool in the warm evening sun.

The evening smells from the orange and lemon grove hung thick in the air, along with the heavy smell of the rich earth beneath them.

I was missing Barbara desperately.

'So?' I asked.

'Well 'tis no secret to yer that there is a million-euro price on yer head,' he began. 'I got distracted with the fact that there could have been a bigger fish to fry. But that one got away. So I'm afraid to say, auld son, that I have to reconsider my options.'

I had to laugh. 'Well, I have to say I've heard a lot about the IRA, but from what I'm seeing now they don't look too dangerous. You couldn't even handle one man and two unarmed women without getting one of you killed.'

Jesús Alcantara looked a little embarrassed.

Dooley couldn't help a wry smile. 'I'll have to give you that one, Jack.'

Johnny McGouldrick, with his everlasting grin, said, 'Girls, can we not talk business tonight? We have a party to get started.'

I lit the barbecue and threw on some pork steaks in garlic for starters.

'So, apart from killing people,' I asked, 'what else do you do?'

He thought about it.

'Not a lot really, and work's a bit short at the moment.'

'He's even working for nothing at the moment,' Johnny McGouldrick laughed.

'What's that?' I asked.

'Danny McReynolds!' howled McGouldrick. 'At Villa Park.'

'That was you?' I said incredulously.

'One of my greatest shots,' grinned Dooley. 'Son of a traitorous bastard. I couldn't get the bastard Sean McReynolds, so I took out Danny Boy. And believe me, Jack, while there's a breath left in me body I'll never stop trying. I'll get the fucker one day.'

So spoke Liam Dooley.

The Executioner.

A chill shiver ran through my body.

Sixty-six

Jane was tormented and confused. She couldn't get out of her head the things that she had been told about David Walker.

But how could they be true?

As she left the bullfight with him, she knew that she would have to confront him.

But how?

What could she say?

She didn't believe it.

So how could she even mention it?

It was just so preposterous. Wasn't it?

Hand in hand, they hailed a local taxi and took it back to his apartment.

Where she would confront him.

Or would she?

Inside the apartment, David Walker said, 'That bullfight was amazing. I had no idea how spectacular it could be. Thank you for taking me. It was one of the most fantastic days of my life. I loved it.'

'I did too,' Jane replied. 'Yes, it was a fantastic day. And it's not over yet.'

She wanted him to take her to bed. But he had to make the first move.

The confrontation that she had planned seemed to be getting sidetracked.

'I went shopping,' David told her. 'I bought lots of goodies. How do you fancy a gourmet evening? I'll cook and cook and cook. And we can drink and drink and drink. A special evening for us. I can cook, you know. And I've spent too much time in hotels. Let me delight you.'

'I certainly like the sound of being delighted,' Jane said excitedly. 'What are we having?'

'First things first,' he told her. 'No good evening should begin without a bottle of Freixenet. It is chilled and waiting.' He filled two flutes and made a toast. 'To my new true friend. Thank you, Jane, for a beautiful day.'

'You're welcome,' she replied and they drank.

'Now, you just make yourself comfortable with the bottle while I lay the table and cook the dinner.'

'I'll set the table,' Jane argued. 'I'd like to help.'

'You'll do no such thing!' he scolded. 'Enjoy.'

She sat on the leather sofa with the ice bucket on the floor as David laid the table.

'So, David, tell me a little about yourself,' she probed. 'I know so little and I am very fond of you.'

'That's a lovely word. Fond,' David said wistfully. 'It reminds me of something my mother would say. Not that you remind me of my mother in any way.'

They both laughed.

He continued, 'I don't wish to sound boastful, because I'm not a boastful person. I have no reason to be. I was fortunately born into money. I do work, but mostly for appearances. I don't really have to. And that sounds terrible, I know. I'm independent. I do some writing and I travel. And while we're on the subject, I'm very "fond" of you too.'

How could she say anything? How could she even ask a question of this lovely charming man?

And he was 'fond' of her too. She pushed all thoughts to the back of her mind.

'I have to work tomorrow,' she told him.

'Yes, I know, I'll get you there. Don't worry.'

He was cooking now.

Giant king prawns in garlic, frying furiously in spattering oil.

It was a smell to die for...

Sixty-seven

The party was going well at the farm. Well, it was difficult to call it a party in the circumstances.

It was early days, and even with my familiarity with death, I was heartbroken. But Barbara was gone. And she wasn't coming back. Another in the trail of dead bodies that littered my past.

When would it all end?

And where was David Walker?

Was he really a murderous psychopathic killer? Or was he what Jane had said, a perfect gentleman?

She was alive, after all.

And nobody had given her a prayer.

Johnny McGouldrick was getting louder. His infectious laugh caught on to us all. 'Haven't ye got any Irish music?' he howled.

'We're in Spain,' I told him.

'Well, have ye got any music at all?' he asked. 'This is a piss poor party!'

That's when I had an idea. I said to my Spanish best friends, Sebastian and Jesús, 'Remember when we hung Mac the Knife we had some flamenco dancers around. Can you still get them?'

Sebastian said, 'I can try. But it's short notice.'

Liam Dooley sat up in his chair. 'Say again, auld son. When you hung Mack the Knife... What's that all about?'

'He murdered my best friend,' I said absently. 'So I killed his gang and his girlfriend, burned down his house, built a gallows in the barn and hanged the bastard.'

'Jesus!' Dooley grinned. 'You don't fuck about, Jack.'

'No, I don't,' I warned him.

'Well, where are the fucking dancers?' howled McGouldrick.

Sebastian made a call.

'Amigo,' he announced, 'the dancers are on the way.'

Dooley and McGouldrick howled and howled and slugged back more Bushmills.

The dancers arrived, with their music.

The guitars hummed like bees, the castanets chattered and clicked: all was joy and music. The Spanish give themselves over to pleasure with admirable frankness, abandon and verve. Their style is typical: the feet hardly leave the ground. It is the body that dances, the back arches, the sides bend and the waist twists with the suppleness of a snake. When she bends over backwards, the dancer's shoulders reach almost to the ground, and the limp, dead arms possess the suppleness and softness of a flowing scarf; however, at the right instant, the leaps of a young jaguar follow after this voluptuous languor.

The frenzied dancers changed from grave dignity to the transports of awakening pleasure, then to languid sensuality, then to an ecstatic frenzy. They finally disappeared gradually into the shadows as the sound of the castanets grew fainter and fainter; then it returned, from afar, growing louder and louder, and exploded completely when they suddenly reappeared in a flood of light.

Jesús Alcantara and Sebastian Aparicio watched appreciatively, clapping with the music. I gazed in fascinated amazement.

Liam Dooley and Johnny McGouldrick stood on their feet, doing their own version.

Which wasn't very good.

But they enjoyed it.

Barbara was never far from my mind. But I tried to push those thoughts to the back of it. I made the decision that tonight I was going to get hammered.

Big style!

And I did.

Sixty-eight

Jane sat with David Walker eating the sensational garlic king prawns and knew that she was falling in love.

She just couldn't help it.

'You are such a wonderful cook,' she enthused. Then she said, 'I'm scared! I'm getting too fond of you. But I don't want to get hurt.'

'I would never do anything to hurt you, Jane.'

But he knew the other fucker might – that wicked bastard in his head.

How could he get rid of him?

'I'm fond of you too. In fact,' he hesitated, 'I don't want to alarm you but I think I may be falling in love with you.'

'Then alarm me, please,' Jane laughed, 'because that's the very thing I've been thinking.'

Their hands crossed the table and met in the middle.

'Steady,' said David, smiling, 'there is no rush. What will be, will be. We have all the time in the world.'

If that crazy fucker doesn't get back in my head, he thought.

'But,' he declared, 'now I must begin the second course. How do you fancy pan fried fillet steak with mushrooms and black pepper sauce?'

'I don't think I like the sound of that,' she joked.

He looked so deflated.

'Don't say that.'

Alarmed, Jane said, 'I was only joking.'

'I know.'

And they both laughed together.

After the conclusion of a fabulous meal, sealed with some Taylor's late-bottled vintage port from the *supermercado*, they sat on the balcony, wistfully holding hands.

Jane wanted this man so badly. She'd never felt like this in her whole life. She was aching for the man. And she'd only known him a few days.

But he was just so wonderful. Well, he had to make the move. She wasn't a tart, and it might look bad if she moved first.

But she couldn't stop the excited tingling between her legs.

And the dampness.

Christ, why didn't he just take her by force?

'Jane,' David Walker said tenuously, 'I'm not sure how to say this.' He hesitated a moment. 'It's just that I have this overwhelming urge to make love to you.'

'Thank God for that! Let's get on with it.'

Without another word they took to the bedroom. They stood kissing gently for a long time. No rush. They began undressing each other until they were both naked. And they kissed some more.

Excitement began to build. They slowly went down onto the bed. David Walker was as stiff as a cricket stump.

Jane was trying her hardest to take it. David was opening her up with his fingers for the moment he hoped she would sit on him. Her suntanned, voluptuous brown breasts dangled and swung. There was only the tiniest patch of white on her body, and that was mostly covered with thick black erotic-looking hair.

She impaled herself on him and he thrust into her. Like a bucking bronco and rider, they began. No thoughts but passion. Inhibitions completely abandoned, they pleasured in the rodeo. Sinking deeper, diving harder. Jane thrust her mouth against David's and took the passionate breath out of his body with her tongue.

They rolled over and he was on top of her.

'Deeper, deeper!' she screamed. 'I'm coming!'

He searched for another inch as they screamed out together with perfect timing.

David Walker had never climaxed like that with a woman in his life.

And never once did he think of killing her.

Sixty-nine

I was waiting at the hotel when Jane turned up for work.

'Where have you been?' I asked her.

'Sorry?'

'You weren't home last night. Where have you been?'

'What's it got to do with you? Are we married or something? I don't even know you.'

'I think you were with David Walker,' I told her. 'And I also think he killed my girlfriend and is a serial killer.'

'You're crazy!' she shouted at me, clearly infuriated. 'You are absolutely crazy. David is a lovely man and I haven't seen him for a couple of days. And by the way, I hardly know him.'

'I think you know where he is. The police need to find him.'

'Then they'd better get looking because I can't help them.'

I knew she was lying.

I left her there at work and drove back to the farm.

The others were there.

'She's lying,' I told them.

Sebastian said, 'The police are looking for him everywhere. It is a massive manhunt, but he has gone to ground.'

'She knows where he is,' I said emphatically.

'I'll have her followed,' Sebastian said.

'Well, after this rejit tipped her off,' piped in Liam Dooley, 'she's not likely to lead you back to him. She's probably warning him as we speak.'

Dooley was right. I knew I'd fucked up.

Johnny McGouldrick stepped in. 'Just be patient, auld son. He has to reappear. It's not so urgent. We kill him this week or we kill him next week. So what?'

Jesús Alcantara was quiet. His wound was painful and I knew he was still hurting from the fact that he had ballsed up with the kidnapping.

His pride was wounded worse than his leg.

As much as she couldn't see it, I knew that Jane was in mortal danger.

David Walker was a psychopathic serial killer, and she was the only one who knew where he was.

They had to track him down. They had to follow her.

He had to be found.

It was then that Jesús Alcantara took the call on his cell phone. From José Miguel Gallega.

Seventy

José Miguel Gallega was no fool.

And he was a very proud man. And he had just rewarded the kidnapper of his wife with 2 million euros.

And on top of that they seemed very much overfamiliar...

The bullfight was sensational.

José Tomas won the day. In the end.

His wife and Doc Holliday and Sonia Carabantes seemed like great friends.

Inseparable.

Almost like lovers!

He was pissed off.

2 million euros pissed off.

Really fucking pissed off.

His Spanish pride seemed to have been seriously damaged. He couldn't have that.

At any price.

He called Jesús Alcantara.

'How is your wound, my friend?' he asked.

'Not so good,' he confessed.

'And the Irishman?' asked Señor Gallega.

'He is good,' Jesús told him. 'Healing well.'

'Good.'

'So.'

'Do you think he would be interested in some work?'

'Well, he doesn't seem too busy at the moment. What is it?'

'Señor Holliday,' said Señor Gallega. 'He has taken me for a fool. You also. And the Irishman. It cannot remain so. He has to be dealt with. I want him taken care of. Permanently.'

'I will speak to him, amigo.'

'Do that, please.'

'Sí.'

'I will pay well.'

The phone went dead.

'Pay well?' Liam Dooley said. 'I was going to do it for nothing.' He rubbed his sore shoulder. 'Any special requests?'

'He didn't make any.'

'Well, tell him that the pleasure's all mine' Dooley grinned. 'And for a million euros he just saved Jack's life.'

'Thanks,' I said.

Seventy-one

They left the bullring in a huge stretch limousine. María, Sonia, José Miguel and Doc.

The cameras flashed as the whole world tried to get pictures of the kidnap victims and their rescuer.

Señor Gallega opened the cava and they all toasted as they drank. They were going back to his fabulous bull-rearing ranch to celebrate.

The *ganadería* was a grand place in a magnificent setting. It was off the coast road overlooking a sea of azure among the orange, olive, banana and prickly pear trees. A vastly sprawling spread of land that reared the finest bulls in all of Spain.

The farmhouse itself was magnificent, with outbuildings all around it. There were corrals with splendid-looking horses snorting and bucking.

Very surreptitiously, María Luisa Gallega squeezed the hand of Doc Holliday.

But not quite surreptitiously enough. It did not escape the attention of her husband as the limousine came to a stop outside the house.

'Señor Holliday,' he said. 'I hope I will be able to repay you with my hospitality for the way you rescued my wife.'

'I'm sure you will,' replied Doc Holliday.

'Señor Holliday,' Señora Gallega offered, 'let me take you for a tour of the ranch before I show you to your room. Can you ride?'

Doc Holliday smiled inwardly. 'Just a little.'

'Then I'll have two horses saddled and I'll show you the sights.' Then, almost as an afterthought she asked, 'Is that all right with you, my husband?'

'Of course, my dear,' he said condescendingly. 'That's the least you can do for your, ah, gallant rescuer. I'll get two horses prepared for you.'

They got out of the limo and Señor Gallega barked some

orders to a leather-skinned worker, while Sonia Carabantes went into the house.

Two saddled horses were rushed over. Señor Gallega said, 'Enjoy the tour, señor.'

Then he entered the house, leaving the two of them to mount up and ride.

Inside the house he used his cell phone to call Jesús Alcantara.

'Amigo. Please remove this piece of horse shit from my life. For ever... Now.'

Seventy-two

'So your man's in a bit of a hurry,' said Liam Dooley.

We were all at the farm, Sebastian, Jesús, Me, Dooley and the ever cheerful Johnny McGouldrick.

'Yes, señor,' replied Jesús Alcantara, gravely.

'Well, I say let's get it done,' McGouldrick said, looking unusually serious. 'Let's do him, and then get the other fucker who cut up Barbara.'

I felt a bit out of it all. As if everybody else was getting some action except me.

Sebastian Aparicio said, 'I think I should alert my cousin at the crematorium. There may be more work for him.'

'There will be, auld son,' Dooley assured him. 'Trust me.'

'So what's the crack?' asked McGouldrick.

Jesús Alcantara told him, 'Holliday is touring the ranch on horseback as we speak with Señora Gallega. José Miguel does not want him to return.'

'Fair enough, auld son,' said Dooley. 'Let's get it done. But this is slightly personal.' He massaged his shoulder. 'It ain't going to be long-range. I want to do it close. Can one of youse drive us?'

Sebastian said, 'It will have to be me. Jesús cannot drive with his wounded leg and I don't want Jack to be involved. If there is a problem, at least as a policeman I have a better chance to clear it up.'

'So let's go!' howled Johnny McGouldrick, throwing down a last Bushmills.

They took the Volvo, Sebastian driving. Dooley and McGouldrick sat in the back. They were obviously talking tactics.

It wasn't a long drive to the ranch. Sebastian had spoken to José Miguel Gallega on his cell phone and knew the rough location of the target. He wasn't convinced the close-up kill was the best option, but he wasn't doing it. A long-range shot would have been far easier, he thought. But…

They were on the ranch now, and taking directions from Señor Gallega. They saw dust in the distance and headed towards it. The two horses and riders were moving slowly side by side.

'Can you get ahead of them?' Dooley asked. 'Without looking obvious?'

'I can try, señor,' replied Sebastian.

McGouldrick was checking his gun. 'So let's get it done.'

Sebastian took a wide detour to get ahead of the horses. It was hot and dusty and the earthy smell choked their nostrils. The car stopped about half a mile ahead of them by some trees. Dooley and McGouldrick climbed nimbly out of the Volvo and went into the trees. Sebastian drove off.

'When they get close enough we'll surprise them,' Dooley told McGouldrick. 'You just make sure you're covering my back.'

'No problem, auld son,' said McGouldrick, grinning.

They waited in the trees as the horses approached. The riders were laughing and talking. As they got close Dooley stepped out. McGouldrick remained hidden.

'Greetings, auld son,' said Dooley. 'We meet again.'

'When did we meet the last time?' Holliday asked.

'On the high seas.'

'Oh yes... I remember now.'

Dooley rubbed his shoulder. 'So do I.'

'The way it goes, I suppose.'

'Swings and roundabouts.'

'So what now?'

'Payback, auld son.'

Holliday shrugged. 'Well, we all have to go sometime, although to be honest if I had a choice this wouldn't be it. But it doesn't look as if I have. So there you go.'

Dooley raised his gun.

'Do you mind if I get off the horse? I don't want to bang my head.'

María Luisa Gallega cried out something as Holliday dismounted.

'You're a cool one for sure,' said Dooley. 'I admire you for that.'

'What must be, must be,' said Holliday. 'I'll move away from the horse. Don't hurt him. Make it clean.'

María Luisa Gallega screamed in terror as Liam Dooley admiringly put three shots into the heart of Doc Holliday.

Johnny McGouldrick emerged from the trees.

'Got some balls, that one.'

Seventy-three

David Walker was also falling in love.

But he wasn't so sure about the other fucker.

The one in his head.

The one he wanted to be rid of.

The one that was destroying his life.

Fucking hell, there must be a way!

How was he to do it?

He didn't know.

He was in despair.

Surely, somehow he could do it?

But how?

He didn't know.

He just knew that he had to find a way to stop the other fucker from killing and cutting up Jane.

He just had to.

Didn't he!

He was thinking all these things when his phone rang.

Jane said, 'I can't come to you tonight. There are some crazy people telling me bad things about you and I think they will follow me. I'm afraid I may lead them to you. I cannot risk that.'

'What things?' David asked.

'I can't talk now,' Jane said, avoiding the question. 'I'll contact you later. But stay in the apartment. Don't show yourself. See you soon.'

Of course David Walker knew 'what things'. They were talking about the fucked-up psycho in his head. The one he wanted to get rid of.

The monster!

He decided there and then to kill the bastard.

Before he killed Jane.

Seventy-four

'It's job done, auld son,' Liam Dooley announced to Jesús Alcantara. 'Can ye tell yer man to get my money and I'll be gone. I'm tiring of this place. I want to go back home. I want to walk in the rain again.'

'I will see to it, señor,' Jesús told him. 'I know it will be here in the morning.'

'Well, *your* business might be concluded,' snapped Johnny McGouldrick, 'but mine surely is not! I swore on me sainted mother's life that I would get the bastard that killed Jack's Barbara, and I will.'

'And good luck to you too. But I'm out of here. I'm sure the four of you can manage it alone.'

'We can,' I said. 'Holliday... what happened?'

They told me.

Sebastian said, 'Two of my men are cleaning him up as we speak. By the morning my cousin at the crematorium will have disposed of him. María Luisa Gallega will never speak of this thing again. It is finished.'

'He died like a man,' Johnny McGouldrick declared, slapping his thigh. 'I think we should drink to him.'

We seemed to drink to anything these days. I passed around the San Miguels and fired up the barbecue.

Liam Dooley was going home, if he could get a plane.

'I've still a little unfinished business,' he explained. 'I have to find a way to Sean McReynolds. He has to be paid back.'

'Why don't you just leave it now?' asked McGouldrick. 'You killed his son on television. Why not just leave it at that? You'd only be putting him out of his misery anyway.'

'I can't. It has to be done,' Dooley said, as if it was some kind of fateful mission.

I thought of Barbara.

And then I thought, Why does killing never end things? It just leads to more killing.

It just never seems to solve anything.

Sebastian said to Jesús Alcantara, 'Your wound, my friend, I can see it is troubling you. I will take you to my friend to fix it.'

Jesús nodded. '*Gracias.*'

'Can I take the Volvo?' he asked Dooley.

'You can have it, auld son. It's all yours. If Jack here will take me to the airport.'

Seventy-five

I took Liam Dooley to Malaga Airport the next morning and said goodbye to him.

The Executioner.

My executioner.

I was glad to see him go.

As I drove back to the farm in the open-top Jaguar I reflected on all that was happening.

There was just the four of us now: Sebastian, Jesús, myself and my new friend, Johnny McGouldrick, who had taken it on himself to seek revenge for Barbara.

As I crunched the car onto the gravel at the farm, McGouldrick was sat at the bar with a beer. It was almost midday and getting hot.

I climbed from the Jaguar. 'Can you fix me a beer?' I called.

'Sure as that, auld son,' McGouldrick called back.

I went in the house and put on a pair of shorts. He met me at the pool with a cold San Miguel. We sat down.

'Yer man Sebastian is having the girl tailed,' he told me, 'but thanks to you he thinks she's on to us.'

I sighed and shrugged. 'I slipped up there. But what's done is done.'

'He'll appear,' said McGouldrick.

'So why are you taking this so personal?' I asked McGouldrick.

'Barbara – she made friends with me,' he choked. 'It was a short friendship, but none the less she was my friend. Somebody killed her and carved her up. You don't do that to a friend of mine... and get away with it.'

I choked up a little and I felt some tears warmly strolling over my cheeks. They landed saltily in my mouth.

I did something emotional.

Something I never do.

I stretched across the table and shook Johnny McGouldrick's hand.

Holding on to it, tears of grief spilled from me and I cried. Uncontrollably.

Johnny held my hand tightly. 'Let it go, auld son,' he told me. 'We'll get the bastard.'

Seventy-six

David Walker decided to move on. He phoned Jane and told her.

'As soon as I know where I am I'll phone you,' he told her. 'I love you, Jane. I want you to join me. Don't worry about your job. I'll take care of you. Be careful. You are probably being watched and followed. When I send for you you must be extra careful. Promise me.'

'I promise. I love you. I'll wait.'

He stole a car.

When he got where he was going he could dump it.

No trace.

The hire car would be safe in the paid for apartment for at least a month.

He chose a nondescript model from a large hotel.

Might not be missed for a day or two.

It had a full tank.

A bonus.

He drove.

Everything changes when you leave the Costa del Sol at the Straits of Gibraltar and travel round the coast to Costa de la Luz. Development stops, the beaches are empty and the countryside takes on a Peak District-like ruggedness.

It is made even more beautiful by the bright light that characterises this coast – indeed, its name means Coast of Light.

The white villages glow against the golden sands and green plains.

Just fifteen minutes from upmarket Sotogrande and San Roque, and an hour from Marbella, the first town you reach is Tarifa, the most southerly town on mainland Europe. It has a relaxed bohemian charm that owes more to Morocco, six miles across the Straits, than it does to the Spanish Costas.

Tarifa is the most cosmopolitan town in southern Spain, yet it retains its traditional *andaluz* charm. It's not a place that appeals to the snowbird crowd who flock to the Costa del Sol.

The hills behind Tarifa are equally beautiful, awash with wild flowers in spring. La Pena, a short drive to Los Lances beach, and El Cuarton, a low-density development which grew in the seventies, are among the most popular rural areas.

There are hundreds of houses hidden in the hills behind Tarifa and Algeciras but more than fifty per cent of them are illegal. Officially the properties don't exist.

It was one of these that David Walker rented in an assumed name before abandoning the stolen car somewhere in the hills.

Seventy-seven

Sebastian Aparicio and all his friends in the Police Force could find no trace of David Walker. Following Jane was getting them nowhere either.

I was impatient and frustrated. Johnny McGouldrick was laid-back about it all. 'Stay cool, Jack,' he repeated. 'He'll turn up eventually.' Meanwhile, Jesús Alcantara's wound was beginning to heal and he felt better.

Barbara was never far from my mind. We all talked a lot about her and it made me feel better. Then I would come over all morose and sink into depression.

It was early days.

We had to find David Walker. Maybe that would help to fix things.

But David Walker felt the urges returning.

He phoned Jane. For her own safety.

'These people you told me about may be following you,' he told her. 'I have found a new place to stay. In a few days you can join me. But you will have to be careful. I'll phone you when it's safe.'

From him!

He had to hunt again...

The bastard in his head needed feeding.

But not on Jane.

Seventy-eight

There is a relatively small British population in Tarifa – most visitors are French because it is the gateway to Morocco, where French is spoken – but there are plenty of beautiful surfer types frequenting the trendy bars and clubs.

It was to one of those trendy bars that David Walker was drawn that evening.

In his suave, handsome manner he sat at the bar with a bottle of wine on ice.

And like a spider he waited for the fly.

His web of mystery captured the eye of a beautiful young girl. She was tanned, with long blonde hair and wearing the shortest of skirts. His eyes were drawn to her sheer top and obvious absence of a bra. Her nipples pressed tantalisingly against the fabric.

David Walker smiled at her and raised his glass. She smiled beautifully back.

Come into my parlour, said the spider to the fly…

She casually moved to the bar and stood by him on his bar stool.

'You are English?' she asked in a heavy French accent.

'I am indeed,' he replied in his best upper-class voice. 'And you are obviously French.'

'Yes, I am,' she said. 'I'm here to surf. But how do you say? I am lonely, on my own.'

'You have come here alone?' David Walker asked.

'Yes, I have,' she told him. 'I am a student and I am travelling around Europe for the summer. And you?'

'I've rented a house in the hills,' he told her. 'I'm writing a book and need somewhere quiet and peaceful. I decided to come into town tonight for a little time out. I'm glad I did.'

'So am I.'

'Would you like some wine?'

'Please. Yes, I would.'

'I'm lonely too,' he confessed.

'Then maybe we should keep each other company for a while,' she said.

'What a lovely idea,' he said charmingly, as he asked the waiter for another glass.

He poured her some wine and they fell into conversation.

She was from Antibes in the South of France. She had arrived in Tarifa yesterday and found a quiet place on the beach to sleep.

She hadn't got a lot of money.

'Have you eaten?' he asked her.

'Not this evening. No,' she replied.

'Would you like to?' he asked. 'My treat for your beautiful company.'

She was flattered.

'That would be lovely. I'm dying for something to eat.'

'Yes, I know,' the fucker in his head told her.

Seventy-nine

After the port he called for a taxi, and hand in hand they were driven to his rented house.

She knew the score.

She'd had a free night, food and drink. She had nowhere to sleep and now she was going to his place.

It was payback time.

She just hoped he wasn't too kinky.

'Who?'

David Walker!

'Kinky.'

He ripped and tore the clothes off her the minute he closed the door. He groped and squeezed her body violently.

Oh no! she thought.

But it was too late now.

The monster inside him had completely taken over.

He was no longer David Walker, he was the fucked in the head psychopathic killer. He grabbed at her ample pubic hair and forced his fingers inside her. He frogmarched her to the bedroom and threw her onto the bed.

'Don't hurt me,' she pleaded. 'I'll do anything you want... anything!'

He took the 69 position and buried his head between her thighs.

'Suck me!' he ordered her. 'Hurt me and you're dead.'

Tears streaming down her face, she cried pitifully, 'I won't, I promise.'

She sucked and heaved and cried until it was over and he fell down on top of her to rest.

But it was only the beginning.

Not the end.

The monster in his head wanted more.

And he wouldn't let David Walker go until he had it.

Quivering with fear and terror, the French girl watched as he slit her throat.

Mercifully, death was swift.

Then he cut back her breasts and slashed open her naval and made a T cut from her vagina.

The monster in his head satisfied, David Walker slept all night with the girl from France.

Eighty

He wrapped the body in sheets and blankets.

He retrieved the undiscovered car he'd stolen and drove it deep into the hills. He found a remote deserted area and abandoned the French girl, covering her with loose stones and rocks.

It would be a long time before anyone found her. If ever.

He abandoned the car for the second time and walked back to his rented house.

He phoned Jane and told her his address.

She would come when she could.

I was getting very impatient and agitated.

Sebastian had one of his police friends constantly on the tail of Jane. She was going about her job as a tour rep as usual.

She took a tour coach into the hills and Sebastian's man followed. It stopped for lunch at a bar in Tarifa.

And then Jane did something strange.

With everybody in the restaurant eating, she took a taxi. It took her to a house in the hills.

David Walker met her at the door and ushered her in.

The taxi waited.

After fifteen minutes Jane re-emerged and got back into the waiting taxi.

She returned to the restaurant in time to meet the tourists for the rest of the excursion.

Sebastian Aparicio was excited as he answered his cell phone.

'I think we've found him, Jack,' he told me excitedly.

'Then let's go and get the bastard!' I snarled with venom. 'Let's get it done.'

Johnny McGouldrick raised his hand. 'Jack, leave this one to me. You're too emotionally involved. You're likely to make a mistake and get hurt,' he said wisely. 'I'll handle it. At the moment you're not as sharp as you need to be. You're vulnerable. Take a back seat.'

'No,' I protested.

'Jack. Trust me.'

I knew he was right.

But it hurt.

A lot!

I wanted to be the one to get David Walker.

But so be it.

Johnny McGouldrick was to be my champion.

Good luck to him.

Eighty-one

'Surprise is the secret to success,' announced Johnny McGouldrick. 'We'll take him tonight.'

Jesús Alcantara volunteered, 'I'll come with you.'

'No you won't!' snapped McGouldrick firmly. 'I don't need a wounded man getting under my feet.'

'I'll come along,' I insisted.

'Jack, auld son,' said McGouldrick, 'I'm not being difficult, but in your state of mind you'd be more hindrance than help. You might get me killed, and there's no way I'm having that. Sebastian here – our fine, upstanding policeman – can drive me there and I'll take care of it.'

I gave in and started to cook some food on the barbecue. We had a few beers.

Johnny McGouldrick took it sensibly.

Business first.

We could celebrate later.

Hopefully...

They didn't speak a lot on the way to David Walker's. Sebastian was concentrating on the driving.

McGouldrick was concentrating on the kill.

It was pitch black as they stopped a good way from the illegal house in the hills. There was a light on.

'No closer,' warned McGouldrick. 'I'll sneak up quietly. You wait here.'

'Take care, amigo,' Sebastian told him, 'he is a very dangerous man.'

'I've shit 'em, auld son,' was McGouldrick's reply.

He got out of the car quietly, not daring to close the door. Stealthily he approached the house.

The curtains were drawn but there was a crack in the middle. McGouldrick sneaked a peek. David Walker was sitting in an armchair with a drink in his hand listening to music.

McGouldrick tried to figure out his next move. He wondered if the door was open. Or a window. He wanted to maintain the element of surprise.

As quietly as a cat he moved to the front door. He tried the handle.

The door was unlocked.

A fatal mistake, he thought.

He quietly entered the hall. The door to David Walker's room was ajar. Holding his silenced Glock in his hand, McGouldrick pushed the door slowly back.

David Walker looked calmly around at him.

'Who are you?' he asked.

'The avenging angel, auld son.'

'Interesting. Avenging who?'

'A friend of mine.'

'Who is?'

'Barbara. You butchered her up.'

'Not me. You must have the wrong person.'

Of course, he was telling the truth. It was the fucker in his head.

Not him.

'So what do you intend to do?'

'Butcher you.'

McGouldrick moved closer holding the gun steady.

'Do you have experience in that department?' asked David Walker.

'Not that much. But I can learn.'

'It takes time, you know,' said David Walker. 'I don't think you have enough.'

McGouldrick didn't even see it coming.

It was so fast and lethal. The scalpel appeared from nowhere and slit his throat from side to side.

It was instantaneous. He knew nothing about it.

He was spouting blood like water from a garden feature.

That fucker in his head came in useful sometimes, David Walker conceded.

He guessed correctly that it was time to get going again.

God, this was getting tiresome…

He left by the back door and for the third time retrieved the stolen car.

Thank God for the full tank of petrol.

Eighty-two

Sebastian Aparicio was getting concerned.

It had been an hour.

There was no sign of Johnny McGouldrick. He knew he'd intended to make the killer suffer, but it seemed a long time.

He decided to investigate.

Entering the house, he was shocked at what he saw.

McGouldrick was lying on his back on the floor, his throat slit wide open and saturated in blood.

It was grim news that Sebastian told me on his cell phone.

Johnny McGouldrick was dead.

Where to next? David Walker wondered.

He was beginning to feel like a fugitive.

That's what he was, really.

A fugitive!

He phoned Jane.

'I'm on the move again,' he told her. 'Some madman tried to kill me. Said I had murdered his friend. I'm scared. I'll contact you soon.'

He drove through the early hours to Torremolinos and dumped the car.

He took a taxi into Malaga and arrived at daybreak, tired.

But a big city, he thought, would be safer.

During Phoenician times, Malaca, as it was known then, was the second most important trading port in Spain, with a valuable fish salting industry from which it derived its name (*malac* means 'to salt'). The Romans created a thriving colony, rich from the good farmland and inland silver mines. The Moors transformed Malaga into the principal port of the Kingdom of Granada and heavily fortified the seafront and town centre. According to contemporary Moorish writers, 'this paradise on earth' was a vital trading centre – busy, populous and extremely beautiful. During the Christian Reconquest the city was besieged for more than 3½ months, finally surrendering on 18 August 1487. The ensuing repopulation by Christian immigrants from the north created economic mismanagement and hastened a decline which lasted until quite recently.

During the last century, Malaga became a popular residence for foreigners, particularly the English.

Eastwards lie the narrow and crowded backstreets of the old part of the town. Malaga is the most important southern coastal town after Cadiz. Bustling alamedas (walkways) and congested backstreets make it quite hectic.

It was here that David Walker found Vince's Bar.

Vince was a cockney expat who'd set up a bar and catered for the English. He was opening for breakfast when David Walker wearily paid off the taxi.

'Good morning,' David Walker greeted him cheerfully.

'Bin travelling long, my mate?' Vince asked in an exaggerated cockney accent. 'You look knackered.'

'I am knackered,' David Walker replied. 'Very much knackered. And hungry too.'

'Well, this could be your lucky day, my son,' Vince told him. 'A very lucky day. You need a room? 'Cause if you do, I've got one free. Right over the bar. A full English breakfast and a clean bed to sleep in, all in one go!'

'Deal,' said David Walker.

Eighty-three

The shocking death of Johnny McGouldrick was just sinking in.

It could have been me!

David Walker was a very dangerous man. And he had slipped away again.

What would Jane have to say now?

I decided to find out.

Sebastian was still having her followed and I knew she was at the hotel, working.

Jesús Alcantara was healing well but still convalescing.

I went alone.

Jane was concluding a welcome party in the hotel lounge when I came upon her.

She didn't look pleased to see me.

'What do you want now?' she snapped. She had already spoken to David on his cell phone.

'The police followed you to a house in the hills beyond Tarifa. David Walker brutally killed my friend. He slashed open his throat.'

'And what was your friend doing there? Did he have a gun, by any chance? Had he gone there to kill David? What was he supposed to do? Just allow himself to be murdered? Fuck off out of my life!'

End of conversation.

With my tail firmly between my legs I returned to the farm.

Jesús Alcantara was still by the pool.

I told him what had been said.

He shrugged, 'I'm afraid, amigo, she does have a point.'

'I know,' I conceded reluctantly.

'We have set ourselves up as judge, jury and executioner,' Jesús said. 'We have no right.'

It was true. It was revenge we wanted, not justice.

'Where will he turn up next?' Jesús pondered.

'God only knows,' I sighed. 'He's a slippery little fish.'

'A dangerous predator, señor,' Jesús said wisely. 'I think we had better start giving him a little more respect.'

'Our best hope of finding him is still through the girl,' I said optimistically. 'She's in contact with him, and led us to him once. She'll do it again.'

'But where did it get us, Jack?' Jesús asked me. 'Just another body.'

Eighty-four

The room above Vince's Bar was spacious and comfortable with an en suite bathroom.

It was cheap too.

And the food from the bar downstairs smelled delicious. The bar itself was clean and well decorated and extremely handy.

David Walker settled into his new residence and phoned Jane again.

He knew she would be followed. He told her where he was and gave her elaborate instructions to follow in order to shake off any tail.

Jane was smart. When she arrived at Vince's Bar there was no one behind her.

'They've lost her,' Sebastian told me. 'In the old town of Malaga.'

'Then we'd better get down there and find them,' I told him. 'She's in serious danger.'

'Amigo, we have done our best for her,' said Sebastian despondently. 'She will not listen. Malaga is a big city, over half a million people.'

'Well, phone headquarters and tell them where he is,' I said, telling him his job. 'Get the manpower. He has to be found.'

'*Sí.*'

The manhunt switched to Malaga. Every policeman had a photo of David Walker. They were showing it in all the hotels, bars and restaurants.

When Officer Miguel Jimenez arrived at Vince's Bar, Vince was in the beer cellar changing a barrel. David Walker was in his room. Sergio Garcia, Vince's barman, shrugged his shoulders and shook his head. Officer Jimenez saluted and moved on.

I drove at speed to Malaga and went straight to the old town, where Sebastian's man had last seen the girl. The narrow backstreets were crowded. It was a warren; I didn't know where to start.

I wandered around aimlessly, thinking it was pretty hopeless. If I found them it would be sheer luck. I went from street to street, from bar to bar, showing anyone that would look a photo of David Walker.

Nobody recognised him.

I stopped for a while in a small bar and had a beer.

I tried to think of something, but knew that all I could do was keep trawling the streets hoping for some luck.

Some hope.

Eighty-five

David Walker opened the door of his room and Jane fell into his arms.

'Did anybody follow you?' he asked anxiously.

'Don't really know,' she replied, 'but I did everything you told me. I dived into the middle of every crowd I saw and in and out of every busy store. I think it would have been impossible to tail me to here.'

'Good girl.'

'What happened at the house?' she asked, sounding frightened.

'I was sitting in the lounge with a drink,' he told her truthfully. 'I heard a sound. I turned around and there was a man in the room with a gun in his hand. He was Irish. He was talking a load of rubbish about how I'd killed a friend of his.'

'I know, I've heard the same rubbish.' She sighed.

David Walker continued, 'I've had some army training. He got a little careless. Talking too much. I had a split-second opportunity and I killed him. It was the only thing I could do.'

'I understand,' she said sympathetically.

'Now I'm in trouble,' he said with an air of desperation. 'Big trouble.'

'Why don't you go to the police and tell them what happened?' Jane asked.

'They'd never believe me. I have to find a way to escape. Get lost for a while.'

'Malaga is a big, busy city,' said Jane. 'You should be all right here for a while.'

'Yes. I was lucky to find this room,' he told her truthfully. 'Do you fancy a drink and something to eat? It'll be quiet in the bar at this time of day.'

'I'm starving,' she declared.

It was four in the afternoon. Vince was having a few hours' rest before the evening crowds came in.

Sergio Garcia was polishing some glasses. He looked up as they came in and sat down. '*Buenas tardes,*' he offered.

'*Buenas tardes,*' David and Jane replied together.

'A menu, señor?'

'Yes please, and two drinks, please. What would you like, Jane?' David asked.

'Beer, please.'

'Two beers please. One large, one small.'

'*Sí, señor.*'

He delivered the drinks and two menus.

'*Gracias.*'

'The steak I can recommend, señor,' the waiter told them. 'It is the finest.'

David and Jane nodded to each other.

'Two steaks then,' David Walker declared. 'Medium.'

Writing down the order Sergio Garcia said, 'Have I seen you before, señor? Your face seems familiar.'

'I have a room upstairs,' David Walker volunteered.

'No, I haven't seen you here before, señor. Maybe some other place.'

'Perhaps,' said David Walker. 'I get around a lot.'

'For sure,' said the waiter, turning to the kitchen.

David and Jane chatted quietly as they waited for their meals. When they arrived, David Walker ordered a bottle of red wine. They ate almost in silence.

David Walker noticed the barman eyeing him curiously as if trying to remember where it was that he'd seen him before.

As indeed he was.

And then he remembered.

The photograph the policeman had shown him in the morning. He couldn't be sure, but it was certainly like him…

David Walker was getting slightly alarmed. A little wary.

The waiter came to the table. 'Is everything all right with your meal, señor?' he asked.

'Excellent,' David Walker enthused. 'The steak is perfect. Have you remembered where it was you know me from?'

He was fishing.

'No, señor. But what does it matter? Enjoy the rest of your meal.'

David Walker relaxed a little.

But Sergio Garcia was thinking that it did matter. The policeman had said that he may have killed someone. He wasn't 'certain' that it was the same man. But he was going to call the police anyway.

I was having a beer outside a bar in the old part of town when my phone rang.

'A barman phoned headquarters to say he thinks a man similar to Walker is in his bar. We are sending some men to investigate.'

'Where is he?' I asked.

'A bar in the old part of town called Vince's Bar. Where are you now, Jack?'

'I'm outside a bar in the old town.'

'Which street?'

I told him.

'You're only a few streets away,' he told me.

'How do I get there?'

He gave me instructions.

I left my beer and hastily forced my way through the people in the streets to Vince's Bar.

I entered the bar and Jane saw me immediately.

She screamed out, 'My God, it's him!'

I made a charge towards him. He sidestepped deftly and punched me with enormous force in the middle of my chest. I crashed onto his table, shattering and scattering plates of food and glasses. He grabbed me by the hair and yanked me back up.

Jane's chair crashed over backwards, and with a terrified scream she smashed against the tiled floor.

Getting my breath back, I managed to connect my fist with the side of Walker's face. He grunted with pain and replied by thumping his fist into the side of my head.

I rocked slightly to one side as he took the advantage. Jane was crying hysterically as she scrambled to her feet among the plates and food and broken glass.

I clawed into David's face with my fingers, trying to push him back. He accidentally stood on his wine bottle on the floor and we both crashed down heavily. We rolled on the floor, scrapping like kids in a schoolyard.

The bar was getting trashed. All the tables that were laid for the evening were spilling glass and cutlery all over the bar. Then David Walker found a steak knife and stuck it straight into my shoulder.

I howled with pain. In that moment he pushed me away, scrambled to his feet and kicked me a couple of times.

In the distance I could hear a police siren. So could David Walker.

'Come on, Jane!' he shouted desperately. 'We've got to get out of here.'

He pulled her by the arm and dragged her roughly through the debris that had been the bar.

Sergio Garcia ducked back into the kitchen where he had been cowering and watching the drama unfold. I struggled to my feet in time to see them charging out of the door into the street.

I followed them as they pushed and shoved their way through the angry, protesting crowds. My arm was bleeding and as I pushed my way after them I was dripping blood onto the furious pedestrians' clothes.

They waved fists in anger and howled at me. People knew we were coming and carved a path for us to let us go through.

Jane was slowing Walker up and I was catching him.

Suddenly he stopped to face me. I kept coming. Then he did the unspeakable. He snatched the walking stick from an old man sending him stumbling to the pavement.

The crowds gasped in horror. Holding the end he ran at me and struck me a violent blow to the wound in my arm. Then, as I spun around in agony, he whacked me across the back, dropped the stick and ran.

I fell to my knees in pain, and as people came to my aid I saw him dragging Jane up a side street.

How are we ever going to stop him? I thought.

He seemed invincible.

The police sirens screamed louder and louder until the car stopped at the pavement next to me and the crowd around me.

But they were too late.

David Walker was gone.

And an ambulance was on the way for me.

Eighty-six

David Walker was dragging Jane, literally, through the backstreets of the old town.

She was screaming.

'This has all gone crazy! Let me go! I can't do this.'

'Can't do that. They'll kill us. We've got to get out of here.'

That was when he saw and heard the Spanish police car. Lights flashing and siren wailing, it screamed to a halt beside him. The policeman passenger jumped from the car and raised his gun to David Walker. He put his hands immediately into the air and surrendered.

The policeman moved cautiously towards him, searching the back of his belt for handcuffs. The second policeman had got out of the car and was moving close. Carefully.

'Turn around, señor,' the first policeman ordered. 'Put your hands behind your back.'

David Walker turned around.

Right around!

With the speed of a cat he smashed his hand into the policeman's face and, snatching the gun from his hand, he threw himself to the ground and fired two bullets into the second policeman. The man crashed back onto the pavement, wounded badly. As the first officer tried to rise, David Walker shot him in the throat, then in the chest.

He was dead, or close to it.

Jane was screaming hysterically. David Walker grabbed her arm and pushed her roughly into the police car.

'Let me go! Let me go!' she yelled in terror. 'This is crazy.'

He slapped her. 'Shut the fuck up and get in the car.'

Tyres squealing, he raced off.

After grabbing the second policeman's gun.

He drove with a vengeance to the outskirts of Malaga.

He needed another car.

He was coming up to a petrol station as a car was pulling out. He put on his lights and stopped the car. Jumping out, gun in hand and dragging Jane, he hauled out the elderly driver and pushed Jane into the back.

The elderly driver was terrified and offered no resistance. David Walker jumped in the car and drove for the hills.

'Please, David, let me go!' Jane pleaded. 'You've just shot two policemen, for God's sake. Let me out. This thing is out of control. I don't know what's happening any more.'

'I can't do that, I'm afraid, Jane,' Walker said. 'We're in this together now. I'm in love with you and you with me. We'll have to do this together.'

'Do *what* together?' she wailed. 'We have no future now. You're a fugitive on the run. I want to go home!'

'That's impossible now, I'm afraid,' he sighed. 'We'll probably die together. But at least that way we'll always be together.'

He was getting confused. Who was actually saying that? Was it him or was it the other 'him' in his head?

'I don't want to die,' Jane declared. 'What in God's name is happening? I had a normal life until a few days ago. Now I'm on the run with a cop killer.'

David Walker ignored her. His attention had been drawn to two horsemen riding abreast with hunting rifles slung over their backs.

He drew ahead of them and stopped the car.

'Don't move!' he ordered Jane. 'Stay in the car. I mean it.'

Getting out of the car, he greeted the horsemen.

'*Hola!*'

'*Hola!*' they called back, reining the horses to a stop.

Producing the police pistol from behind his back, David said simply, 'No need to be alarmed. All I want are your rifles and ammunition. Hand them over, and you can be on your way.'

Both men raised their hands. One said, 'No problem, señor. I have another one at home.'

'Just be careful,' Walker warned. 'I'm a nervous man.'

'So are we,' the rider replied.

Carefully they removed the rifles from their backs and the ammunition belts from their waists.

'Please lower them slowly to the ground,' Walker told them. 'Then turn around and ride away the way you came.'

They did what he wanted.

And waited for the bullet.

It never came.

David Walker wasn't a cold-blooded killer.

Was he?

He only killed in self-defence.

The other fucker in his head was the cold-blooded killer.

Wasn't he?

Eighty-seven

Sebastian Aparicio collected me from the hospital.

I was all right. Just hurting a bit.

'Jack,' he told me, 'he has killed two policemen. This is now the biggest manhunt in all of Spain.'

'He still has the girl?' I asked.

'*Sí*,' Sebastian sighed. 'Witnesses say he was dragging her, screaming, through the streets.'

'She should have listened to me,' I told him despairingly.

'I know, Jack. But she didn't. Now I think unfortunately that it is her funeral.'

'Where do you think he's gone? I asked.

'To ground, for sure,' he told me earnestly. 'I don't think he'll pop up again soon. The only lead we had before was the girl. But now he has her. We've no one to follow him. What drives him? What makes him do these things?'

'He has to be psychopathic,' I said. 'He has to be schizophrenic. Two people. One good, one bad, maybe?'

'I'll check with headquarters,' Sebastian said. 'Get the latest update.'

He used his cell phone.

'Two hunters on horseback were robbed at gunpoint,' he told me. 'The description matches Walker. He stole their rifles and ammunition. He didn't harm them. They were shaken up a bit. But thankful for their lives.'

'Sounds like he's preparing for a siege,' I told Sebastian.

But he already knew.

'But where, Jack? Where is he?'

'Could be almost anywhere,' I told him. 'All I know is that he is smart. And dangerous.'

Eighty-eight

'David, if you love me, please let me go,' Jane pleaded. 'I can't do this thing. It's close to crazy.'

'It'll be all right, Jane,' David Walker assured her. 'Trust me. We'll get through this thing. Together.'

'I don't want to get through "this thing" together. I want out. *Now.*'

'Sorry, babe. But you're in.'

He drove the car mercilessly through the barren landscape, not really knowing where he was going.

He had no real purpose other than the fact that he thought the further he got away then the better it would be.

That's what he hoped.

He still loved Jane.

But he thought she was being a little disloyal.

He didn't like that.

Typical woman...

Selfish.

Just thinking about herself.

He drove on.

Looking for something.

Anything.

He didn't know what.

Until he found it.

Se Vende, the board said.

The farmhouse looked deserted.

He drove slowly and quietly into the yard.

It certainly looked uninhabited, but he was taking no chances. Taking the keys to the car with him, he reconnoitred the place.

When he was certain he kicked in the front door.

Eighty-nine

There was no one in the house.

He checked every room carefully.

Jane followed him in, cautiously.

She was frightened.

David Walker inspected the cupboards in the kitchen. There was food in tins, tea, coffee and powdered milk.

He examined the fridge-freezer. There was plenty to feed them for a long while.

'Does someone live here?' Jane asked nervously.

David Walker looked serious. 'I don't think so. But we can't be certain. It doesn't have that lived-in feel. The sign says it's up for sale, and I think the owners have left. Maybe they rented it for a bit. I'll put the car in the garage and we'll have no lights on tonight. We'll have to be cautious.'

'David, this is madness,' Jane tried to reason with him. 'We have no chance.'

'Don't be so negative,' David Walker told her. 'We can lie low here until the heat cools down, then drive to a small fishing village and steal a boat and go to Morocco.'

'You don't fucking get it, do you?' she seethed. 'I don't want to go to Morocco. I want to go home!'

'Unfortunately, that's our only chance now,' he told her.

'No, it's *your* only chance,' she retaliated. 'I've done nothing. You've virtually kidnapped me. I'm a hostage!'

'I'm sorry you see it like that,' he retorted. 'I thought you were in love with me.'

'So did I, until this total madness erupted!' she told him back. 'You just killed two Spanish policemen, for fuck's sake. Can't you see that has to change everything?'

'It doesn't change the love we have for each other.'

'*Had!*' she screamed into his face hysterically. '*Had!*'

212

'Everything will be OK,' he said calmly. 'You'll see. We'll get to Morocco and everything will be fine.'

Then Jane lost it.

It was sheer frustration.

She burst into tears and screamed hysterically, 'I don't want to go to Morocco!'

'Then die here,' the voice in his head said aloud.

Jane felt gripped by panic and fear.

'It'll be all right,' said David Walker.

'Perhaps,' said the voice in his head.

Ninety

I was hurting a lot.

Battered, bruised and beaten.

I'd been defeated in a straight fight with David Walker.

My pride hurt too!

I sat by the pool at my farm, nursing the pain and wondering about it all.

Jesús Alcantara sat close to me, nursing his own wounds.

We shared a bottle of Freixenet, and were both silent.

David Walker had been too good for us.

And where was he?

Was Jane still alive?

Who could tell?

The questions mounted up, with no answers.

I heard the sound of a motorcycle coming down the track.

It was Sebastian Aparicio. He stood the bike and took off his helmet and gloves.

'*Buenas tardes.*' He greeted us both. It was late afternoon. 'He has disappeared, amigos. Again. I don't know how he does it.'

'Sheer determination,' I told him. 'Desperation. Call it what you like, but he doesn't give up easily.'

'*Sí*, Jack, I know,' Sebastian replied. 'The police are swarming the area where he was last seen. Unfortunately it is vast. They are knocking on the door of every home. If there is no answer, they are breaking in. I fear there are going to be many unhappy people.'

'So be it,' I said, 'he has to be found.'

'*Sí.*'

Jesús Alcantara spoke for the first time. He said, 'The area he is in is a good base to get him to Morocco. He has to get out of Spain, and that seems to be his best bet. If I were the police I'd be watching every small fishing village and the whole coastline. It wouldn't be difficult to steal a boat and get across the straits.

Especially for a man with the resources of David Walker. But I don't think he'll try it for a bit. I think he'll hole up for a while and try to let things quieten down.'

'I agree with you, amigo,' said Sebastian Aparicio. 'In fact I will alert headquarters to what you have said. I'm sure they will be very interested.'

I was beginning to feel quite useless. Not like me at all.

But none the less it was a fact.

And I didn't like it.

Ninety-one

The two people that were David Walker were confusing each other.

The real David Walker, who loved Jane, was upset by her apparent disloyalty.

The other David Walker, the stranger who lived in his head, wanted to rape, murder and cut her up.

It was a constant battle to satisfy them both.

But who would win?

The real David Walker was angry with Jane. But he was still in love with her and would never harm her.

Yet the hound in his mind was baying for blood.

But he fought it bravely and decided to win her around.

He put his arm tenderly around her and kissed her softly on the forehead.

'I love you, Jane,' he told her lovingly. 'We can be happy. Relax and unwind. I'm going to cook us a meal. We can chill out together. Leave it to me.'

'OK, David,' she said, all the fight leaving her. 'Whatever you say. Can I help at all?'

'No, my love,' he told her. 'But there's red wine in the kitchen. You could open a bottle and set the table. Just relax.'

Relax. That was a fucking joke! How can you relax with a murderer, for fuck's sake?

But she had no choice.

She played the game.

After all, her life could depend on it.

The wine was good.

The meal was OK, considering what they had to cook with.

David Walker was the perfect gentleman again.

Almost as if everything was normal.

He sipped his wine and said, 'I'm sorry it's not up to the usual standard. I did the best I could with what I had.'

'It's lovely, David,' Jane said, humouring him. 'It really is.'

'I suggest we should take a shower and have an early night,' said David. 'I think we need to rest and unwind. We've had a hectic time of it.'

Jane couldn't argue with that. She was drained. Maybe she was being too hard on David. After all, he'd been forced into his actions.

He was protecting her, after all.

Wasn't he?

Of course he was.

She knew that.

Didn't she?

Ninety-two

The lovemaking was sensational.

David Walker surely knew how to satisfy a woman.

And right now Jane needed satisfying.

Lots of it!

Her whole life was in turmoil because of this man. So she might as well make the best of it.

And she did!

Screaming with ecstasy as he repeatedly plunged into her, she forgot about the anguish of the last few days.

And enjoyed…

But David Walker was still at war with the voice in his head.

He was battling seriously for Jane's life.

That fucker in his head was demanding her life.

Well, he wasn't getting it.

Was he?

No! He fucking wasn't!

When they both climaxed together, he thought the battle was over. But it wasn't.

The other one wanted death and blood. But David Walker fought him and denied him.

He lost.

And David collapsed onto Jane and rolled to the side of her and into her loving arms.

They drifted into a peaceful sleep.

Happily in love.

Together.

Ninety-three

It was the key in the lock and the door opening that woke them.

Someone was in the house...

David Walker shot out of bed at the speed of lightning. He snatched the police pistol from the side of the bed and, ignoring his nakedness, he moved quietly to the bedroom door.

'Don't make a move or a sound,' he warned Jane. 'Stay in bed.'

He slipped out of the room to the top of the stairs.

He heard voices. A man and a woman. Stealthily, he crept down the stairs.

Gun ahead of him.

They were in the dining room.

'What are you doing here?' demanded Anna Lorente, the estate agent who was showing around her German client.

It was the gun that frightened her. Not the fact that the gunman was naked. In fact she found him excitingly handsome and fit.

David Walker knew what he had to do.

He shot the German dead with a bullet to the heart. He crashed backwards onto the floor. Anna Lorente screamed with terror, her hands going to her face.

'Stop screaming this second or you will get the same!' David yelled.

She fell silent in a second.

Perhaps it might have been better for her if she had kept on screaming.

Ninety-four

The police were visiting every fishing village along the vast coastline, however small. They warned everybody to be vigilant and alert. To report anything strange. They passed out thousands of posters with David Walker's face on them, and also a picture of Jane that they had acquired.

Nobody had seen them, but the instant they did they would call the police. David Walker was dangerous, they were told, and under no circumstances should they approach him. Keep a special eye on all boats.

He might try to get to Morocco.

We held another meeting in the bar by the pool. It wasn't one of the best evenings Spain can offer. It was raining lightly and there was a slight chill in the wind. But it was nice for the garden, and the orange, lemon and lime groves.

It changed the whole smell of the farm. The dampness changed the scent of the fruit. You could almost taste it in the air. The damp earth was tangible. You could savour it. The rain danced on the pool and glistened like tiny glass balls in the light around us.

It was serene, calm and beautiful, and a welcome change.

We drank San Miguel from the bottle and enjoyed.

I sat behind the bar.

Barman.

Jesús Alcantara and Sebastian Aparicio sat facing each other on bar stools.

'Smoke?' I asked.

'Sí,' they replied together.

I opened a packet of five White Owl sweets. Not large cigars, but just a nice size. I flicked open and lit my 18-carat gold Dunhill and we sucked on the flame. After settling the cigars and having a few puffs, I sighed. 'No sign of him?'

'Nothing, Jack,' said Sebastian. Then he went on to tell me

what was being done and the plans that were being made. It was a huge manhunt. Spain was in shock. Black armbands were being worn at all sporting events. A minute's silence was being observed everywhere.

'We will find him, Jack,' Sebastian said with conviction. 'There can be no escape for this man.'

Jesús Alcantara took up the conversation. 'We have said that many times before, amigo. But still he eludes us. Every time.'

I drank some beer and sighed. 'He's right. He's had military training. Special Forces, I'd guess.'

'And so have we, Jack,' replied Jesús Alcantara.

'*Sí, amigos!*' Sebastian grinned. 'And look what he did to you.'

We all laughed wryly.

'Thank you for reminding me,' I told him.

'*De nada.*'

'I wonder if Jane is still alive,' I said, exhaling cigar smoke.

'I have a feeling she is, Jack,' Sebastian said thoughtfully. 'I feel she is different, this one. She has survived too long. All the other ones were killed immediately.'

'I think she is different also,' said Jesús. 'You don't think she could be helping him, do you?'

Nobody spoke.

We had all had the same thought at the same time.

Breaking the silence, I said, 'It has to be a possibility, I suppose. But he was seen dragging her screaming through the streets.'

'Or helping her, maybe,' suggested Sebastian Aparicio.

Ninety-five

The voices in his head were raging now.

Demanding it!

Blood.

Jane was locked in the bedroom.

David Walker had ripped the clothes off Anna Lorente. She stood naked and quivering in the living room. Sobbing tears of terror.

She knew she was going to die.

She just knew it.

She just hoped it would be quick.

It wasn't.

David Walker…

No, not David Walker, he told himself.

It was the fucker in his head.

Not him!

But he couldn't stop him now.

He was out of control.

The rape was hard and brutal. Anna Lorente put up no resistance.

She was sobbing prayers. Asking God to forgive her her sins, begging him to welcome her to eternal life. To free her from this monster.

The scalpel flashed over her throat.

And mercifully she was free.

And with the God who welcomed her.

Then her killer butchered her.

When he woke in the morning he was shocked at what he saw.

But he knew he had to clear up the mess, so he set about it. He hid the two bodies in the rear laundry room. But he couldn't get rid of all the blood.

It was impossible.

When he'd done his best he went to Jane.

He had showered and was still naked.

He pushed open the door and stepped in.

From behind the door she crashed a solid onyx table lamp over his head.

And ran for dear life.

Ninety-six

The pain in his head was awful. The blood was caked hard in his hair. He didn't know how long he had been out.

About an hour, he figured.

That fucking ungrateful bitch! After all he had done to save her... and this was how she repaid him.

Well, she was on her own now.

She could die.

He was protecting her no longer.

The fucker in his head could have her.

Outside it was a wilderness.

Jane had no idea where she was. Only that she had escaped. From him.

She was running, scared and breathless. Terrified he would find her. For she knew what he would do. She hoped she'd killed him. But suspected that she hadn't.

Maybe she should have hit him again. And again. Caved in his skull. Made sure.

But she hadn't.

And now she was terrified he would come for her.

She was on a dirt road. Out in the open. She needed to find cover. Somewhere to hide.

A sign of life. That's what she needed. But where?

Fear gripped her. Tightening her body. She kept looking back, fearing what she might see.

There were trees up ahead. She reached them and hid. And rested. Breathing heavily, part in exhaustion, part in terror. She tried to calm herself. She felt safer, not being in the open.

She was on a dirt road. But every road led to somewhere. Hiding and watching, she saw the lights of a car coming from the direction she had come from.

Was it him? Or was it rescue? How could she possibly know?

She could be safe.

Or she could be dead.

She took no chances.

She watched the car crunch dustily past.

Shit.

Shit, shit, shit.

It wasn't him.

She could have been safe.

But she knew what she had to do.

Make it alone.

And she would.

David Walker stocked up the car with the stolen guns and ammunition and all the food and drink from the farmhouse and a few cooking utensils.

He set off to find her.

But where?

He drove the car, slowly from the farmhouse to the road, and stopped.

Which way?

If she had gone left, then he was heading back the way he had come. To trouble.

If she had gone right, then at least he was heading away. From trouble.

He went right.

Jane, of course, didn't know it, but when she went left she had saved her own life.

She heard the music first.

Flamenco music...

Then the lights and the sound of laughter. As she got closer she saw the coaches and the fire. And a pig rotating slowly above it.

She wept, and ran into the arms of the first person she saw.

Ninety-seven

'She's alive!' Sebastian Aparicio put down his mobile phone. 'They found her. She escaped from him.'

'Where is she?' I asked excitedly.

'Rancho Grande,' he replied, 'where they hold the pig roasts for the tourists. The police are on their way to collect her.'

'Well, I tell you now, Sebastian, I'm going after him. He butchered Barbara and beat the shit out of me. I want him. I want him bad. Are you with me?' I asked him.

'Sí, Jack,' he answered. 'I want him also.'

'Jesús?' I asked.

'For sure I'm with you, Jack,' he told me, 'but I'm still hurting a bit. I'm not fit.'

'I know.'

'But I've been worse.'

'I know.'

'I can still fire a gun.'

'Sebastian,' I said, 'find out everything you can at headquarters. Try to talk to her yourself. Get every detail you can. We've got to get this bastard.'

'Sí.'

'I'll speak to my friends at ETA,' volunteered Jesús Alcantara. 'They will get us everything we need: guns, ammunition, anything. Just tell me what you want and I will get it.'

'Make no mistake about it,' I told them both, 'David Walker is a dangerous and ruthless man. He's resourceful and will be hard to hunt. But hunt him down we will. Sebastian, get on to headquarters and find out all you can.'

Sebastian phoned me on my cell phone. 'There are two more bodies, Jack.'

He told me the details.

'I have all the information available. He's trying to get to Morocco.'

'Then we have to try and stop him,' I told him.
'*Sí*, Jack. But how?'
'I don't know that yet.'

Ninety-eight

She had got away.

He knew that for sure. By now she was probably with the police and telling them everything she knew.

They would probably have found the two new bodies and would be intensifying the hunt for him.

They would guess that he was heading for Morocco and would seal it off to him.

But he would find a way. He always did.

He drove high into the hills. As far away from civilisation as he could get. He could easily survive for as long as it took. He knew that. He had warm clothing, food and drink. He could see things out until he had an opportunity.

Patience. That's all it took. It was cold and dark in the hills at night. He was looking for somewhere off the beaten track. The road had deteriorated to rubble and stone. There was a large outcrop of rock by a small stream, where crystal clear water rolled down from above him. He drove behind the outcrop by the steam and parked his stolen car.

It was a sheltered spot where he could light a fire without it being seen. And there was fresh water too. He got out and looked around. The moon was full and bright. The landscape was lit as if by a powerful light bulb.

He started collecting dead dry wood and leaves for his campfire. He was going to enjoy the peace and simplicity of life for a while. It was lovely just being safe and alone in the wilderness of the mountains.

He got a blanket from the car and built up his fire and lit it. It was warm and welcoming, he opened a bottle of red wine with his Swiss Army knife and wrapped himself in the blanket by the campfire.

He drank straight from the bottle. It was good Spanish plonk.

More for reassurance than need, he had the Spanish hunting

rifle by his side. He wasn't in the mood for food but still felt hungry. He searched in the back of the car and found a tin of beans. He opened it with the penknife and forked out the contents.

It was food. It filled him. No more than that. He slugged more wine from the bottle and began to relax a little. He felt safe and warm. It would be hard to find him if he lay low. And he was good at that.

He'd been a survival trainer in the army. All he had to do was hold out until he found a way to Morocco.

And he would.

Ninety-nine

The fire had died out to grey ash and dust.

When David Walker opened his eyes, the sun was climbing tall into the sky. He felt so good that he couldn't describe it.

Freedom!

He stripped naked and washed in the stream. He rinsed out his clothes and lay them across the rocks to dry. He felt like a wandering cowboy discovering Arizona.

He was thinking breakfast.

He followed the stream up until he found a small rock pool. In it were a few trout lazily resting. He only needed one. He lay on his back by the side of the pool and slowly and quietly slid his arm into it. With the gentlest of motions he rubbed the underbelly of a fish. Seemingly unsuspecting, it luxuriated... until with lightning speed David Walker flipped it out of the water beside him. It thrashed for a second until he hit it over the head with a stone.

Breakfast!

He took it back to his camp and gutted it. He relit the fire with fresh dry wood. He dredged mud from the bottom of the stream and covered the fish entirely in it. He dried it in the sun and when it looked like a baking brick he lay it in the fire to bake. When he guessed it was done he flipped it from the fire with a stick. He broke open the parcel with a stone. The skin stayed on the mud to reveal the steaming pink flesh.

David Walker scraped the delicious fish from its skeleton then turned it over and ate the other side.

This is the life, he thought.

He decided to explore his new home. Leaving his clothes to dry in the sun, he took his rifle and went back upstream. He was already well tanned and had no fear of burning.

The landscape was spectacular. Green trees and shrubs and bushes everywhere. He could hide here for ever. And love it.

It was nearly midday and the sun was hot. He leaned down and cupped a handful of water from the crystal clear stream.

It was at that moment he felt the eyes upon him. He looked up and gazed back into them.

They stared each other out.

David Walker slowly lifted his rifle and fired.

One Hundred

We had all we needed.

Guns, ammunition, explosives and grenades.

Jesús Alcantara had seen to that.

Sebastian Aparicio had all the latest intelligence on where David Walker could possibly be.

Not enough, unfortunately.

But we set off anyway.

The manhunt began.

But where was the man?

We drove to the farm where the bodies had been found and where Jane had escaped from.

We tried to think.

Like David Walker would!

The hills to hide out, and then Morocco.

Morocco was nine miles away across the straits. A dead easy trip for someone like David Walker.

I decided that there was no point trying to find him in the hills. He was too smart.

We needed to think like a fugitive and figure out where and when to find a boat.

But how do you do that?

We got the maps out and studied the coast.

Sebastian and the Spanish police were guarding every port and fishing village. But how long for?

Resources came into everything. Eventually they would tire of it.

David Walker could afford to wait.

He was in control.

Again.

He was really pissing me off.

Big time!

One Hundred and One

The rabbit died instantly.

Shot through the head.

Well, that was the evening meal sorted out, thought David Walker. He could live off the land for ever. He could afford to wait. No need to take unnecessary risks.

He was enjoying the peace and solitude. And he noticed that, with no distractions, the voices in his head had nothing to talk about.

He felt calm.

And a little bit sad.

For the rabbit.

After all, it was only being friendly.

But he had to eat. He crossed the stream and picked the rabbit up. Opening his knife, he slit the belly.

It steamed.

He reached inside and removed the heart and liver. While they were still warm, he ate them. Good nourishing food. He didn't skin the rabbit but took it back to his camp and kept it in the cool stream held down by a stone.

It would stay fresher like that.

He lay in the shade of his rocky outcrop and took stock of his situation. It was good, he thought. Time was on his side and he was happy. There was plenty of food to be had, and he had everything he needed to survive in the car.

He sought out the car's jack handle, and with the aid of some small Y-shaped branches, he made a spit over the fire ready to roast his rabbit.

His clothes had dried but he didn't need them. The freedom of being naked in the sun was wonderful. He decided to have a drink. Among the haul of drink from the farm was a bottle of Spanish brandy. He rooted out a glass from one of his bags in the back of the car and poured a couple of fingers.

He drank and immediately felt the spirit work.

Morocco could wait.

This was the life.

They could all wait.

He knew they were looking.

But it was his game.

He skinned his rabbit and poked the jack handle through it and lit his fire. He rotated it over the burning embers, and sipped brandy.

The night began to fall, so he wrapped himself in a blanket as he cooked. The darkness closed in, making the fire glow brighter. The rabbit rotated and spat into the fire. The air was still and the sky was clear. The moon shone and the stars twinkled.

His rabbit was done.

It was time for some wine.

Red, with game.

Of course!

One Hundred and Two

It had been an idyllic week.

The rabbits, wild birds and fish were plentiful.

The solitude and peace of mind had left David Walker content. He was resting up in the sun and planning his escape to Morocco.

He was sure that every town and village on the coast would be guarded. But he didn't need a town or a fishing village. Just one boat. Surely he could find an isolated villa on the coast with a boat moored…

That was his plan. In about another week, he guessed, the Spanish police wouldn't spend much more time or money on him. Eventually they would have to decide that he had got away.

He still had plenty of food and drink in the car and the weather was great. He had built a small shelter with branches and blankets to sleep in at night. He had collected a large supply of firewood and, as another night drew in, he lit his campfire and began roasting today's rabbit impaled on the car's jack handle. He opened a bottle of screw-top Spanish plonk. Red. It was acceptable, considering.

He poured some into his glass and turned the rabbit. It got dark quickly in the hills.

And he was thankful for it.

He seemed at peace.

No voices.

Why?

Maybe no temptation?

Perhaps he should forget Morocco and stay in the hills.

But no!

Eventually he had to get back to civilisation.

He knew that.

And what it meant.

One Hundred and Three

Ramón Furio and María Fernandez were in love.

They were married.

But not to each other.

So they stole every moment they could.

To be together.

Ramón had a boat – a thirty-foot cabin cruiser that he kept moored at an isolated makeshift jetty along the coast where they could meet and make love.

David Walker had come across it on one of his reconnaissance trips.

He made his plans.

He watched and waited.

When everything was ready he made his move.

They never noticed him slip aboard the boat. They were too busy in the throes of passion.

David Walker watched for a while and began to realise how long it had been since he'd done it himself.

He felt aroused.

And something must have aroused the fucker in his head, because he woke up and started talking to him again.

Now he was all confused again.

It was Ramón Furio who saw him first.

And the gun.

María Fernandez looked great naked. She was on top. Her brown bottom stared at him and he could see the huge bush of black pubic hair hanging down. Her huge breasts dangled onto Ramón's chest.

Ramón wilted and dropped out of her.

'Stay where you are!' David Walker ordered her. 'Don't move.'

Menacingly, he held his gun on her and moved closer. He let his trousers fall, and fully armed, drove into her as she straddled her lover.

They were powerless, as weeks of frustration emptied into María Fernandez.

Ramón Furio cried with the pain of it.

This was the woman he loved.

Defiled before his very eyes.

He could take no more.

Pain, anguish, shame, hatred. It overcame him.

The boiling anger could be held in no more.

He threw María Fernandez to one side and lunged at David Walker's throat.

The bullet made a neat hole in his forehead. It didn't bleed a lot.

María Fernandez collapsed from shock.

And David Walker mutilated her.

He was back.

One Hundred and Four

Morocco!

The Straits of Gibraltar, the legendary Pillars of Hercules, are all that separate northern Morocco from Europe. This wild land of green mountains, towering cliffs and deserted beaches seems a world away from the arid expanses of Morocco to the south. The northern coastline, once inaccessible and underdeveloped, is rapidly becoming one of Morocco's most popular destinations, praised for its clear waters and Mediterranean climate.

It was here that David Walker found himself as he took a fire axe and smashed a hole in the boat to sink it.

He swam to the shore, pushing and dragging his large canvas holdall with him. He could only travel with essentials: two pistols, two rifles, ammunition and a small amount of food and a few spare clothes. He felt the sand under his feet and walked through the surf up the beach.

It was 1 a.m. and dark, so he found cover in some trees and decided to sleep. He lay down on the soft sand and ran through in his head everything he had learned from a guidebook on Morocco that he'd found at the farm.

He wasn't very far from Tangier; perhaps five miles. An easy walk in the morning. He planned there to steal a car and drive south-east to the Rif.

The Rif, a chain of spectacular mountains, stretching 300 km to the Algerian border, is traditionally the wildest place in Morocco – the *Bled es Siba*, or 'ungovernable land'. Riffian tribes have always been fiercely independent. Prospective conquerors, from Romans to a succession of Moroccan sultans, have constantly failed to gain a foothold in this barren landscape.

Al-Hoceima, the biggest resort on the Mediterranean coast, enjoys a dramatic setting – a huge bay backed by cliffs enclosing a magnificent white sand beach. The small fishing village has been overtaken by tourist developments which welcome mainly French package holidaymakers.

It was there that David Walker had decided to go.

One Hundred and Five

The news of the two missing people and the disappearance of the boat had to mean only one thing.

David Walker had made it to Morocco.

We had packed the Land Rover Discovery with everything we needed for a long manhunt.

Sebastian, Jesús and myself sat outside a small pavement bar in Tarifa, looking out over the straits to Morocco.

We drank large cold beers in the late afternoon sun.

It was Sebastian who spoke.

'He will be a hard one to find, Jack. For sure he is a dangerous man.'

'And resourceful too,' I said, almost admiringly.

'A bit too resourceful for my liking,' added Jesús Alcantara, taking a long drink. 'What next?'

'We'll stay here tonight,' I told him, 'and get on the first ferry to Morocco in the morning. That's the first place to start.'

'The Moroccan police are being cooperative,' Sebastian informed us. 'They are sympathetic that two of our officers were killed. Also, they don't relish the idea of a madman on the loose in their country. They are prepared to turn a blind eye to much of our activities – within reason.'

'So what can they tell us?' I asked him hopefully.

'There's been no sign of him, Jack,' Sebastian said gravely. 'But two bodies were washed up on the shore. The man was shot in the head. The woman was severely cut. Mutilated. Investigations discovered that they were both Spanish.'

'That's him, the bastard!' raged Jesús Alcantara. 'Jack, we must find this fucker and kill him like the dog that he is. The trail of death is endless. And Barbara…'

'Yes, I know,' I sighed sadly. 'I know. But we'll get him.'

One Hundred and Six

Stealing a car in Tangier had been easy.

He drove through the Rif on the main road and was soon in Al-Hoceima. He made his way to the older part of the village and found a quiet side street to park the car. Taking his holdall from the back seat, he wandered down to the port.

It was ten o'clock and he was hungry. He found a pavement café and ordered breakfast and a beer. It was warm, and the view of the fishing boats bobbing on the water was calming.

He needed accommodation.

Something small and cheap where he could fit in as a traveller. Not too many questions. Just cash money. He paid in euros, which the waiter seemed more than happy to take. He enquired about accommodation and was given a recommendation. He tipped the waiter well and thanked him.

It was budget accommodation: a hostel (*riad*).

The old woman in reception had skin like an old crocodile wallet he had once owned. He was certain that she had never been pretty even sixty years ago. She showed him to his room, which was immaculate and whitewashed and very basic.

It had a small private bathroom with no plug, thanks to the Muslim tradition of washing under running water. He thanked her and she shuffled slowly away.

He put down the holdall and noticed that there was no minibar!

'So what am I going to do now?' he asked himself.

He washed and shaved and changed into the only change of clothes he had. He locked his room and pocketed the key to go and explore the village. As he passed her, he thanked the crocodile wallet, who smiled and revealed that she had the matching teeth.

Attractive.

He went shopping.

Clothes, shoes, a bottle of Jack Daniels and a map of the area.

He changed into his new outfit in the fitting room where he bought it, and the helpful assistant disposed of the old one.

Feeling human again for the first time in weeks, he found a decent restaurant and ordered a top-class meal.

The pretty Scottish waitress who served him was working her way around the world.

He was charming and he made her laugh.

She liked him.

David Walker liked her too.

And so did the fucker in his head.

One Hundred and Seven

We took the first ferry from Algeciras to Tangier. It was a short journey and soon we were driving off into the North African port.

There are two types of police in Morocco – the Gendarmerie, dressed in khaki with green berets, and the Sûreté Nationale, who wear grey. The Gendarmerie deal more with internal security, while the Sûreté Nationale carry out local policing in towns and are responsible for tourists.

It was they who met us and steered us quickly through all the formalities. Sebastian Aparicio did all the talking. Jesús and myself stayed back. After half an hour, Sebastian and the policemen casually saluted each other and Sebastian returned to the Land Rover.

'I've given them the photo of David Walker,' he told us. 'They are going to circulate it.'

'Do they have any information?' I asked him.

'Possibly,' he answered thoughtfully. 'A car was stolen early in the morning on the night the boat and the Spanish couple disappeared. It may be a coincidence, but surprisingly cars do not get stolen here very often.'

'What are they doing about it?' asked Jesús Alcantara.

'They have circulated the number and are looking out for it,' replied Sebastian. 'Now listen to me carefully. This is a very delicate situation. Officially we are not here.'

'So how does that work?' I asked him.

'They are very sympathetic to the fact that we have lost two comrades,' he said seriously. 'After all, we are all policemen doing our job. Spain has officially asked Morocco to try and apprehend and arrest him.'

'So where does that leave us?' I asked again.

'If we find him first and he should be killed, they want us to get rid of him,' Sebastian said gravely.

I sighed as I said, 'I have to admit that sounds a bit bizarre.'

'This is Morocco, Jack,' he replied somewhat menacingly. 'Officially, he is not even here. If he is never found then he was never here.'

Jesús Alcantara said thoughtfully, 'I am beginning to understand. If we can exterminate this vermin quietly we do everyone a favour.'

'Exactly,' said Sebastian, a sly grin spreading across his face. 'The police will help us as much as they can with information, but will try not to get physically involved. If they were to arrest him it would cause all sorts of problems. It is best if he never turns up.'

'So we can "unofficially" officially kill him.' I smiled. 'I said it was bizarre.'

'The officer's words, not mine,' said Sebastian. ' "Sweep him up like the dog that he is and dispose of him." '

'So where do we start?' Jesús asked. 'He could be anywhere.'

'The officer said that if he were him he would head towards the Rif,' Sebastian told us. 'It is a lawless area with many small towns and villages. Fishing villages also. Where you could steal a boat, perhaps.'

'So do you think we should go that way,' I asked, 'and hope for the best?'

'The police are concentrating on that area to try and find the stolen car,' Sebastian informed us.

'That's if it was him who stole the car,' I said sceptically.

'It's the only clue we have, Jack.'

'Maybe he is in Tangier.'

'Perhaps.'

'So maybe one of us should stay here,' I argued.

'I think the car is the best bet, Jack,' Sebastian argued back. 'He likes the wide open spaces.'

'So be it,' I said, giving in.

One Hundred and Eight

David Walker was walking back to Crocodile Wallet's hotel when he saw the Sûreté Nationale examining the stolen car. He ducked into an alley. One man was on his radio, the second officer had the door open and was examining the inside.

Not good, thought David Walker. They might just have spotted the stolen car or they might be looking for him.

He couldn't take the chance.

He found another way to the hostel.

The leathery old woman flashed her crocodile smile. He smiled back.

Perhaps she fancied him.

He went to his room and collected his holdall. Still with his shopping bags, he regretfully informed Crocodile Wallet that he had to leave. He paid her handsomely.

But she still looked sad.

'I'm so sorry,' he told her.

Where to next? A boat, maybe? But there was no point stealing one. It just led them back to you.

This is Morocco, for God's sake. There has to be a crooked boat owner interested in making some money...

He wandered carefully around the backstreets looking for somewhere to hide. He found what looked like a disused area behind the boatyards.

There were lots of sheds, some with doors, some without. One or two had broken boats in them. The smell of decay stung his nostrils. A couple of cats roamed in search of food. A dog barked at him warily. He passed from shed to shed until he found one with a filthy, dusty old car in it. He didn't know what it was but when he tried the door it opened. It had two large comfortable leather bench seats.

And it was clean inside.

Home sweet home.

He put his holdall and shopping in the back and took out one of the handguns and checked it was fully loaded. He tucked it inside his trousers and reached into one of the shopping bags for the JD. He pulled out the stopper and took a large swig. He climbed into the front and got comfortable.

He would rest until dark.

In the meantime the two Sûreté Internationale officers were following the instincts of good policemen. If you had travelled all night, stolen a car and driven a long way, you were going to be hungry. So they decided to check all local bars and cafés, showing every bartender the picture of David Walker. It wasn't long before one bar owner recognised the picture.

Yes, he remembered the man well. He tipped well and asked if he could recommend some decent cheap accommodation.

He told them where he had recommended.

They phoned headquarters.

Headquarters phoned Sebastian Aparicio.

Sebastian Aparicio told me and Jesús Alcantara.

We were on our way.

One Hundred and Nine

He was gone.

The weathered old woman told me sadly that he had left almost at the same time that he had arrived.

He must have been spooked.

But how?

By what?

'He can't be far,' I announced to Sebastian and Jesús.

'He's a smart one, Jack,' said Jesús Alcantara, 'and cool too. He's always ahead of the game.'

Sebastian said, 'I think we are closing in on him. He is running scared.'

'Running maybe,' I said, 'but not scared. I don't think he scares. He's been trained too well for that.'

'*Sí*, Jack,' said Jesús with a very serious tone in his voice. 'He is a very dangerous man and we must be very wary of him. He kills cold-bloodedly, without mercy. We must be so careful if we find him. If you think he is dangerous now, think how he would be as a cornered rat.'

I felt a slight shiver of fear and apprehension. I almost felt like I was having a bad premonition.

Sebastian snapped me out of it. 'We need to split up and scour the town. He is still here somewhere. He will stay aground until dark. He won't move around by day. Let's rest, have something to eat, and tonight we'll trawl the town.'

We all agreed.

It was the rat that woke up David Walker.

It was in the car.

A fucking rat!

He hated rats.

He kicked out at it and it scarpered, squealing.

He felt the sweat of fear.

Scared of a rat!

For fuck's sake.

It was dark.

Pitch black.

He slugged the JD.

Scared of a fucking rat…

He couldn't believe it!

He shuddered.

And took some more JD.

He changed his shirt for a loose-fitting one he had bought that afternoon, which he could wear outside his trousers to hide the gun.

He left the comfort of his new home and wandered off. He intended to steer clear of any tourist or brightly lit areas. He was keeping to the Moroccan quarter.

The streets were dark, dangerous and menacing. He followed his ears to the sound of traditional Moroccan music. There was a bar ahead of him. As he entered, he realised it was much larger than it appeared from the outside. It was thick with smoke, and full of men jabbering away, laughing, smoking and drinking. Some were in traditional costume, some not. They all looked surprised to see him, but not unduly concerned. He weaved his way through the smoke and the tables to the bar.

In his best British accent, he said, 'Good evening, gentlemen. Nice evening. Can I order a large beer, please?'

He always found that his best British accent threw people worldwide.

'Are you lost, my friend?' asked the man behind the bar.

'I'm not really going anywhere in particular, so how could I be lost?' David Walker smiled. 'I could certainly do with a beer, though.'

The bartender poured a large beer and put it on the counter in front of him. 'We don't get many British in here.'

'Well, I'm sure that my money is as good as the next man's. Will you join me for a drink?'

'It would be inhospitable of me not to, my friend. Of course.'

He poured some brown spirit into a tumbler. He raised it. '*Choukrane*,' he said (Thank you).

They both drank.

The slight tension in the room evaporated.

'How did you find my place?' the bartender asked.

'I was just wandering around and saw it,' David Walker replied casually.

'Not such a good idea, my friend.'

'I can take care of myself.'

'I hope you can.'

'I can. Have you any food I can order?'

'Goat stew and fresh bread.'

'Sounds marvellous! I'll have some.'

'There are no tables.'

'I'll eat it at the bar.'

'I'll get you some.'

'Thank you very much.'

One Hundred and Ten

The goat stew had been good.

After a few more beers and the brown stuff, David Walker explained that he was being pursued by dangerous men and that he needed to get out of Morocco.

He wanted a boat with a captain who would ask no questions. He could pay well.

His new best friend knew the very man. So, armed with the name of the boat and the skipper, he began carefully tracing his way in the shadows towards the harbour.

The closer he got, the brighter became the lights. Going as carefully as he could, and keeping as much to the shadows as he could, he reached the harbour. Following the instructions he had been given he found the forty-foot sailing boat.

There were a few lights on as it bobbed up and down on the gentle swell. There was a short gang plank to the deck. He stepped onto the deck and knocked gently on the cabin door.

After a few wary questions and answers, David Walker entered the cabin and closed the door behind him. Half an hour later, after a couple of glasses of the brown piss, the deal was done and he left the boat. He was back on the quayside.

I was cruising at walking pace in the Land Rover when I saw him. I pulled into the side. I phoned Sebastian and Jesús.

'I've spotted him,' I told them quietly. Why quietly, I didn't know. 'He's on the harbour. He seems to be working out which way to go. Get down here quick while I track him. This might be our only chance.'

It was darker by the water. More shadows. He didn't seem eager to cross the street to where the bars and shops were. He seemed cool. Unhurried. The further he walked, the darker it was getting. He was heading to the edge of town. The shops and bars on the other side of the street were thinning out.

There was a rap on my side window. I looked down; it was

Sebastian and Jesús. I motioned to them to get in. Jesús got in the back while Sebastian ran round the back and climbed in the front.

'Where is he?'

'Just down the…'

He was gone.

For fuck's sake!

In a few seconds he was gone.

I drove quickly to where he had been just in time to catch sight of him on the other side of the street. He did a left. I hurled the Land Rover dangerously across the traffic, scattering vehicles wildly. Furious drivers blasted their horns, screaming and hurling abuse.

They all managed to avoid me. The tyres screamed as I slammed the Discovery up the road that David Walker had taken.

He must have heard all the commotion because he turned and stared back at me. He was no fool. As I bore down on him he coolly took out his gun, took careful aim and shattered my windscreen.

The Discovery veered out of control from one side of the street to the other. I smashed a small parked car to pieces before Sebastian Aparicio kicked out the shattered screen showering us in glass.

I saw the grin on David Walker's face as he raised the gun again to fire. Just the sight of it was enough to send me careering wildly away from its aim. I smashed another car to scrap metal and veered back towards him.

Sebastian took a wild shot and hit something twenty feet away. An alarmed motorist skewed to a halt in the middle of the street. David Walker ran to the car, yanked open the door and threw the driver to the road. In a second he was in the running car, flashing past me in the opposite direction. I slammed the car into reverse and, tyres screaming, managed to turn around and chase after him.

Back at the main harbour road, he hurled the car out into the scattering traffic. I followed after him, colliding with two cars that bounced away into other cars, which in turn smashed into other cars.

Glass, metal, tyres and sparks, like fireworks, were left behind me as I chased in wild pursuit after David Walker. Pedestrians fled in terror. He was heading for the docks.

David Walker had a plan. He hammered the car onto the dark wooden pier and aimed it towards the end.

There was a gap between two boats before the end of the pier. He flung open the door of the car and rolled out onto the pier, under the rail and splashed into the water.

The car roared on to the end and, headlights blazing, launched itself into the air and smashed violently into the water.

David Walker swam to some steps on the pier wall and stealthily sneaked up to the top, just as I roared past him.

I stopped at the end of the pier a hundred yards away.

One Hundred and Eleven

David Walker knew that he was the hunted and they were the hunters. Without them chasing him he could get free.

Nobody else was really that bothered.

He decided to try and cut down the odds.

On his belly, he carefully snaked along towards the three men standing at the end of the pier, staring into the water.

'Well, he hasn't come up.'

'Was he ever in there?'

'Someone was driving.'

'He could have dived out.'

'He might be swimming back along the pier and getting to the road.'

David Walker didn't know who was saying what.

Nor did he care.

If he could just get one, he had cut the odds by a third.

Any one would do. He couldn't hope for better than that. Get one and get away.

He slipped the gun from his belt. He was close enough now.

He planned his escape in his mind. He knew that surprise would give him that precious advantage. He was thirty yards from them. He didn't need to get any closer.

He was a first-class marksman.

Resting his elbow on the ground and supporting himself with his left hand, he took aim at the man in the middle. He knew that both men on the outside would turn in towards him to help. That would give him the precious seconds he needed to escape.

He fired twice into the back of Sebastian Aparicio, who crashed forward onto the pier.

David Walker bolted like a hare.

We fell to our knees on either side of Sebastian. I looked up as Jesús examined him. I saw David Walker running down the pier.

'He's dead, Jack. Let's get the bastard!'

We gave chase.

My God, he was fast.

The soft life had taken its toll on us. He was getting away, but we still had him in sight.

David Walker could easily have got away. But he was letting them follow him.

Into a trap.

They would never give up. He knew that. So he wanted to end it tonight.

One way or the other.

He was making his way to the disused sheds and garages behind the old boatyard. It was pitch-black there but it gave him the advantage.

He knew the layout.

They seemed to be slipping behind a bit. He didn't want them to lose him. He slowed down. Just a bit.

He had led them into the trap. He had reached the yard. He shuddered as a few rats appeared. A wild feral cat pounced and bit into the neck of one of them. It squealed as the cat bit deeper and ran off with it.

David Walker shuddered.

He saw his home ahead of him. Now was the time to lose them. He ducked here, ducked there and ducked everywhere until he slipped unseen into his shed.

Now they would have to seek him out.

Cautiously.

From inside the shed he had a good view of the surrounding area. He wound down the front-door window of a car and opened the door fully. He took one of the hunting rifles from his holdall and checked it was fully loaded. He rested it on the window ledge of the car door and sighted down the barrel from side to side.

He couldn't possibly miss a clear target from here.

An evil grin spread wickedly across his mouth.

All he had to do now was wait.

We stopped just short of the yard and sheltered behind a stinking dumpster.

'I don't like this,' I said anxiously. 'I feel a little vulnerable. Trapped.'

'I understand, Jack,' Jesús said to me. 'We must be very cautious. He could be hiding anywhere. Or he could be escaping.'

'He's such a fox,' I confessed. 'He scares me.'

'Me too, amigo.'

'I think he wants a showdown. Get it over with.'

Jesús Alcantara sighed deeply. 'I think you are right, Jack. What shall we do?'

I hesitated slightly, then said, 'We have no choice, we've come so far.'

'Sí.'

'We'll have to spread out and be careful.' I swallowed, dry in the mouth.

'Good luck, amigo.'

'You too, my friend.'

David Walker took some JD from the neck of the bottle. His cat's eyes, well accustomed to the dark by now, scoured the area in front of him. He was looking for the slightest movement and listening for the lightest of sounds.

There were none.

Then, the very tiniest of movements caught his eye. It was not much more than a sense. But enough to alert him.

High alert.

He readied the rifle on the car-door window and concentrated one hundred per cent on the open area in front of him.

Jesús Alcantara was nervous. Scared, even. He didn't like this situation at all. His mouth was dry. The palms of his hands were sweating. He hadn't felt like this for a long time. David Walker had got him rattled.

His gut instinct was to turn around and go home.

He felt ashamed.

Snap out of it!

David Walker had just killed his best friend.

He had to avenge him.

But something inside told him that David Walker was in a different league.

But why?

Who was he?

255

And where did he come from?

Jesús crouched fearfully and moved infinitely slowly forward, alert to every sound and movement. His breathing was heavy. He could hear his heart pound against the wall of his chest. He wanted to turn and go back.

But what would Jack think?

Probably nothing.

But…

David Walker had picked up on the shadow advancing slowly towards him.

He homed in down the barrel of the rifle on the target. His finger was on the trigger. He sighted on the chest. The target was crouched.

Be patient.

Wait.

Wait until he raises himself slightly.

Patience.

Patience.

His finger pressed the trigger.

But not too much.

The target rose to step over something and David Walker's finger gently squeezed.

The shot rang out.

Jesús Alcantara didn't hear it.

He felt the impact as it hurled him backwards.

He was dead before he smashed into the empty oil drums behind him.

Two down, one to go, thought his killer.

One Hundred and Twelve

I heard the shot and the ensuing noise.

It was to my right.

I was filled with fear and panic. It wasn't a pistol shot. It was a rifle shot. And I knew that David Walker had robbed two Spanish hunters of their rifles.

Powerful rifles.

I crept as quietly as I could in the direction. I was aware every second that David Walker was waiting for the slightest sight of me and was ready to shoot.

The deserted yard was an eerie place. It was dark and scary; the palms of my hand were sweating. I could feel my heart thumping. In a low voice I called, 'Jesús, can you hear me?'

There was no reply. I snuck about, trying to maintain cover wherever I could. I peeked around the side of a shed where there was a little open ground.

My heart sank.

Lying motionless face down was Jesús Alcantara. There was a large hole in his back from the exit wound and his shirt was saturated in thick coagulating blood.

I felt grief beyond belief. Another life, another friend, lost. And for what? The revenge for Barbara. Is this what she would have wanted?

I didn't think so.

It had all seemed so easy at first. We would hunt down this dog and kill him. Get our revenge and feel better for it. But we made the fatal mistake of underestimating the enemy.

And we had paid for it!

Well, it was up to me now. It was me against David Walker. One on one. And the best man would win. I could see that Jesús was plainly dead, and as much as I wanted to, I couldn't go near his body. I knew that would be suicide. There was a rifle out there somewhere trained on that very spot.

But where?

I needed to draw his fire without getting myself shot.

Crouching low, I ran towards Jesús and threw myself to the ground just as the shot went off and smacked into the oil drums I had landed behind. The drums banged out a tune as the spent bullet ricocheted around inside.

I'd just caught the flash and had sight of his hide. Not that it helped a lot. With only a handgun there wasn't much chance of storming the place. Watching the dilapidated shed, I decided to rest.

I had to try and get him out in the open. This was going to be my one and only last chance. I dare not fail. Barbara, Sebastian, Johnny and Jesús were dead because of him.

And also partly because of me. I know we all went into it with our eyes open, but just the same I was the last man standing and I had to finish it.

And I would, I told myself.

I hatched a vague semblance of a desperate plan. I didn't think David Walker would desert the safety of his hideout. So, keeping cover, I rummaged around the yard, searching every shed looking for something that might help me.

I picked up an old jerrycan and shook it. There was a drop in the bottom. Not much, but a start. I found a beat-up abandoned old speedboat in one shed, and a small red can which held maybe an inch of fuel in the bottom. I poured it into the jerrycan. After scavenging all over for about half an hour I had collected maybe two pints of fuel.

Not much, but enough to start a fire.

I made a wide circle around the yard until I was behind the shed that I hoped David Walker was still in. As silently and as stealthily as a cat, I crept to the back of the wooden building. The untreated wood was as dry as tinder.

I'd picked up an old rusty can from the floor, beans or peas or something. I filled it from the jerrycan. It would be easier to splash it evenly all over the back and sides of the shed. It was great. I threw it halfway up and it ran down evenly. I felt more confident and in control now.

The adrenalin began to pump. Let's see you get out of this,

you crafty little bastard, I said to myself. I wanted to be around the front when it went up, so I needed a slight delay. Just a couple of minutes. I built a small pile of wood about a foot from the building and shook the last drops of fuel onto it. I knew that when I lit it I would have a few minutes before the flames leapt across onto the building.

I lit the fire and when I was confident I speedily took the long and safe way back to the front of the hide.

David Walker smelled it long before he saw it. He knew what it was of course. Fire. He had expected something but was never quite sure what it would be.

Good thinking. Just the sort of thing he would have done himself. Well done. Calmly, and without panic, he searched around for something that might help him. Standing against the wall was a sturdy solid oar to a rowing boat. It was heavy. Using it like a lance he smashed it through the side wall of the building. Then again and again, until the hole was big enough for him to climb through.

He dashed into the darkness as the fire took hold. It roared and crackled. Flames leapt high into the sky.

David Walker screamed in pain. As loud and fearfully as he could. He sounded in mortal agony.

'Help me, help me please!' he screamed. 'Mercy, mercy! God have mercy!'

The sound was pitiful. He was burning up in agony in the throes of death. The screams became shrill and then started to fade to a moan.

Then silence.

Just the sound of a raging inferno. The roof caved in. The walls collapsed. It was now a funeral pyre.

David Walker was dead.

It was over.

One Hundred and Thirteen

I tucked the handgun inside my belt and stepped out from my cover. Jesús Alcantara, one of my two best friends, lay dead on his face in front of me. He was in a rather grotesque position; his arms and legs were twisted all over the place.

He couldn't possibly be comfortable, I thought, in some kind of a crazy trance. I turned him over and straightened him out. I put his arms by his side and shed some tears.

The building was glowing hot embers now. You could feel the intense heat even here. I thought about what to do next.

It was a mess. The whole thing was a huge fucking mess. I'd almost forgotten about Sebastian in all the excitement. That poor bastard was lying dead on the jetty, and God only knows what was happening back there.

My mind began to clear a little and I knew I would have to phone the local emergency services. I reached in my pocket for my cell phone.

'Not a bad effort really,' said David Walker, holding a gun on me. 'It might have worked with most people. Surely you didn't expect me to come running out of the front door. Jack, really!'

I was shocked with disbelief. I just stared at him.

'I'm sorry, Jack, but I think this is the end of the road for you,' he told me grimly. 'It was a good chase but I think the best man won in the end.'

I tried to take it on the chin but it wasn't easy. My mind was racing to think of a way to jump him and get the upper hand. I told myself that I wasn't beaten yet. Not by a long way. Just let him do the talking. Action speaks louder than words.

'I need to keep this short, Jack, I'm afraid,' he told me. 'As much as I would like to talk to you. I feel I need to get away from here. Your bonfire is going to cause a lot of interest.'

I thought of lunging straight at him or grabbing for my gun. What was there to lose?

'Jack, I have to go. I have enjoyed our meetings.' It sounded final. 'But I'm going to spare your life. Out of some kind of respect. But I have to leave a little token you can remember me by.'

He shot me in each shoulder and once in the leg.

'Goodbye, Jack,' he said, and disappeared.

I crashed to the floor in agony as I just caught a glimpse of his back.

David Walker was running back towards the harbour. He knew where he was going: to the boat and the captain he had spoken to earlier. The lights and the town were getting closer. There was furious activity around the harbour.

Police lights flashed, ambulance lights flashed and people were running everywhere. It was chaos all over the place.

That was good.

Good for him, anyway.

He ran to the boat's berth.

It wasn't there.

There was a man on the deck of the boat next to it.

'The boat that was here,' he called. 'Where is it?'

'Gone to sea, my friend,' the man called back.

David Walker leaped from the jetty onto the deck of the startled man's boat.

David Walker held his gun on the frightened man and told him calmly, 'I will spare your life, I swear it on my mother's grave, if you get me away from here. I am a man of my word.'

'I believe you, my friend,' he said calmly. 'I seem to have no choice. I must put my faith in God. And your word.'

Epilogue

Since the death of Danny Boy – the new George Best – Sean McReynolds had lost all interest in living.

He discharged himself from the Witness Protection Programme and prayed for the day that Liam Dooley would come for him and put him out of his misery.

That day had come. Dooley took aim with his long-distance sniper's rifle and, getting McReynolds in the cross hairs, he gently squeezed the trigger.

In the split second that it took the bullet to pass through his head, Sean McReynolds found time to thank his killer.

He was out of his misery.

Out of the worst nightmare of his life.

He was free.

Thank you, Liam, auld son.

The pain was finally over.

María Louisa Gallega devoted her life to her husband, José Miguel Gallega, and tried to set aside the vision of her lover, 'Doc' Holliday, being shot to death in front of her.

She was a Spanish noblewoman and always would be. Her husband was a rich and powerful man.

She loved him dearly.

It wasn't her fault that she had been kidnapped and raped. She couldn't imagine life without him.

Doc Holliday was dead, and she would never again give him a single thought.

Would she?

David Walker was true to his word and spared the boatman's life. In fact he paid him too. The boatman was relieved and grateful.

He set him ashore on the Costa del Sol, also known as the Costa del Crime.

Lying low and finding contacts in the underworld, David Walker got a new passport and melted off the face of the earth.

He was free to carry on his life in peace.

He found a café where he took a shine to the young waitress. Czech. Very nice.

I remembered the words of Jesús Alcantara. 'When the rain has fallen, señor, there is no way that you can put it back in the sky.'

I lay in hospital recovering from my wounds. I thought about our disastrous pursuit of vengeance. How we thought we were invincible.

And then I remembered the wise old words of my grandfather.

'Son,' he told me, 'it doesn't matter how hard or tough you think you are, there is always someone harder and tougher than you.'

I thought about it and just hoped that one day David Walker would meet that man.

The End

Lightning Source UK Ltd.
Milton Keynes UK
24 September 2009

144136UK00001B/9/P